Yougga Finds Mother Teresa

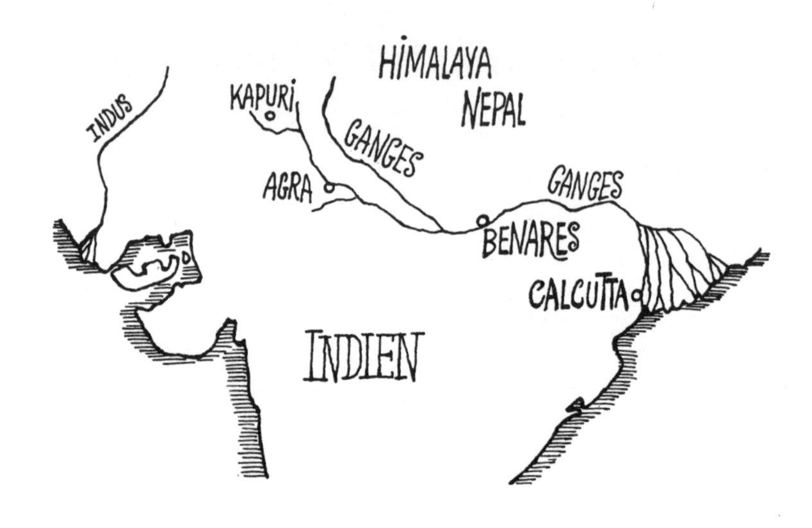

THE SEABURY PRESS · NEW YORK

Yougga
Finds Mother Teresa

The Adventures of a Beggar Boy in India

KIRSTEN BANG

Translated from the French by Kathryn Spink
Illustrated by Kamma Svensson

1983
The Seabury Press
815 Second Avenue
New York, NY 10017

First published in Denmark in 1977 by "Abbe Pierre's Children's Aid" Mother Teresa's Co-Workers in Denmark.
English translation first published in Great Britain 1983 by Element Books, Ltd.

Printed in the United States of America

Library of Congress Cataloging in Publication Data

Bang, Kirsten.
Yougga finds Mother Teresa.

Translation of the work orginally published as: Tiggarpojken, Jugga.
Summary: Traces the adventures of a crippled beggar boy on a pilgrimage to the Holy City of Benares, then on to Calcutta, where he encounters Mother Teresa and benefits from her compassion for the poorest of the poor.
1. Teresa, Mother, 1910- —Juvenile literature. 2. Children—India—Juvenile literature. [1. Teresa, Mother, 1910- 2. India—Description and travel. 3. Nuns. 4. Missionaries. 5. Poverty] I. Svensson, Kamma, ill. II. Title.
BX4406.5.Z8B3613 1983 271'.97 [92] 83-4267
ISBN 0-8164-2469-1 (pbk.)

Contents

Dedicated to all the children who help Mother Teresa

For many years schoolchildren in Denmark have been sending milk to the children of India. In 1972 this delightful book was written and published in order to help the Danish children to understand better the life, customs and traditions of India.

Much of the milk is sent to the little ones looked after by the Sisters and Brothers of the Missionaries of Charity, the Order formed by Mother Teresa of Calcutta. Mother Teresa has involved children all round the world by appealing to them to help their young brothers and sisters who are hungry in India. Many children from Scandinavian countries (including the Faroe Islands) regularly send milk powder, condensed milk and baby foods, those from English-speaking countries send flour for bread, and German-speaking children provide vitamin pills. A bond of love and concern has been formed between children throughout the world.

Mother Teresa's message to all the world is a message of love . . . understanding love . . . for those in need — "the least of my brothers". The story of the valiant Yougga, the young beggar-boy and those he meets, is told with just such understanding love.

May God bless the children of India, and those who wrote, illustrated and translated this book, the Missionaries of Charity, and all the children of the world — all those who are united by the works of love, that through such links of love may flourish peace and joy.

ANN BLAIKIE
International Link
International Association of the Co-Workers of Mother Teresa

I *The Village*

Nirad, the shoe-maker's son, pushed his boat through the rushes, moored it to a rotten post and waded ashore. He was carrying a net with six shining fishes wriggling in it. He was very pleased with the day's catch. Sometimes he caught nothing at all. As he limped along the rough path between the green flooded rice fields back to the village, the straw-roofed houses were visible between the coconut palms at some distance from the river.

The shoe-maker's son — the name had stuck with him despite the fact that he had long been an adult. No doubt this was because he had never married. Who would want a semi-hunchback with a limp who could hardly provide for his old mother? Nirad, for his part, had always been on his guard against women. He was a little afraid of them and thought they were dangerous and demanding. They wanted this and they wanted that. Then came the children, a succession of mouths to feed, commitments and criticism. Why don't you work for the planters? Why don't you make sandals like your father? He was a good shoe-maker, he was! Why don't you repair the goat's shed? The wall collapsed in the monsoon rains years ago. Why don't you fill in the hole in the straw roof of the back room?

In the beginning his mother had talked to him like that too, but gradually she had gone quiet. She had been such a good woman. Then suddenly, one evening she had collapsed onto her bed and died. Tears welled in Nirad's eyes at the very thought of it. The dear old woman! How he missed her. Why had she left him so soon? He couldn't get over it. He would never get over it.

He thought of her as he made his way home across the fields as he had done so often since she had died. How happy she would have been to see him return with so many fishes. They would have eaten two of them straight away for supper, put two on one side to dry and given two to the woman next door in exchange for flour. His mother would have lit the fire immediately to cook the fishes; she would have kneaded flour, water and salt to make "chapatis" in the flat iron cooking pot and then they would have eaten together, squatting opposite each other on the covered terrace which opened out on to the street, the cooking pot between them. His mother really used to know how to make life pleasant.

Perhaps he should have tried to find himself a wife anyway but it wouldn't have been easy. And who after all could replace his mother? Young girls didn't seem to be interested in much except silver bangles for their ankles and coloured glass bracelets; where could he find the money for those kind of useless things? His mother now — she had admired him, loved him and made excuses for him when others criticised him. No, life had hardly been worth living since she had left him.

Nirad felt sorry for himself as he hobbled home on his long thin legs, one of which was slightly shorter than the other; the net full of fish knocked against his dirty loin-cloth which had at one time been blue; it was now so faded and filthy that it wasn't any particular colour. His mother had always washed his clothes — he must remind himself to swill them through next time he went down to the river.

Nirad's home was in the outermost street, the street where the shoe-makers, tanners and sweepers lived. At one time the outcastes, the untouchables, the pariahs had made their homes there, but all that had been abolished by a law; there was no longer any difference between the castes.

And yet on the whole it was still the same people who lived in his district; they did the same jobs and lived in the same little mud houses built one up against the next to prevent them from falling down.

All the same, some progress had been made, thought Nirad, who was old enough to remember the day when the town-crier proclaimed throughout the village that

India had now become independent and that all the differences between the castes had been wiped out.

Now the children of the pariahs could go to school with all the other village children, even with the children of the Brahmins. Even if it didn't very often happen, at least they had the right to do so. And everyone could go into the temple in the square, whereas not long ago the pariahs had had to remain outside and be content to glimpse from a distance the beautifully decorated images of the gods: the golden Siva with his trident and his wife, the black Durga, with her eight arms. Not that the former pariahs went to the temple very often. After all they had their own goddess, Kengamma! She stood under the banyan tree by the pool and even those who were not outcastes visited her from time to time with offerings of flowers and rice, because everyone knew that she was the village's own deity. Siva and Durga were great and powerful and were worshipped throughout the country, but it must not be forgotten that this village had always belonged to Kengamma. For this reason also the outcastes' district was held in a certain regard, for it was here that Kengamma lived!

Nirad limped past the pool and glanced at the crumbling statue standing there in the shadows among the climbing roots of the tree. Then he arrived at his dark empty little home. He sat down on the narrow covered terrace which opened on to the street. Beyond it there were two small windowless rooms. The one at the front was not much bigger than his bed which just squeezed into it. From the back room a door led to the courtyard with the tumbledown goat's shed and a little kitchen garden; the herbs had half-withered, the onion tops were trailing on the ground, the tomato plants were yellow and limp; his mother had always watered them. Nirad often forgot about that kind of thing — he sighed.

He must light the fire for himself. He still had a little wood but no cow dung. That always made the fire glow. Tomorrow he would have to go out into the fields and find one or two pats. Then he would have to mould the dung into shape himself and slap it on to the wall of the house to dry. It was not dignified for a man to have to do women's work. When his mother was alive there had always been little round cakes of cow dung on the wall of the goat's shed in the courtyard at the back.

The family next door — the man was a tanner — were just gathering for their evening meal. The woman was cooking rice in a pot while the man squatted on the ground, smoking his hookah which made a gurgling

The woman was cooking rice in a pot while her husband squatted on the ground, smoking his hookah.

sound with every puff. Some of the children were playing in the gutter in front of the house. The poor tanner already had six children, three of them girls, and his wife looked very much as if she was pregnant again. No, really, life was very much better without a wife and marriage. He would rather contend with his own loneliness.

Warm pungent smoke was rising from all the small fires where people were preparing their evening meal; blue clouds of smoke drifted down the narrow dusty street, darkness was beginning to fall and the temperature had dropped — now was the best time of the day.

"Did you catch anything today?" asked the tanner over the small wall which separated the two terraces.

"Six enormous trout," announced Nirad proudly. "Would you like to buy some?"

The woman looked enviously at the fish — it would make a pleasant change from endless boiled rice with vegetables.

"A cup of rice for one and a cup of flour for the other," Nirad dangled his net in front of the tanner and his wife. "Choose for yourself." They had no flour left but they would manage a cup of rice.

The tanner succumbed to temptation and selected the two largest trout, and Nirad put one fish on to cook for himself. The other three he would clean and dry so that they would keep and he could sell them.

The tanner's wife called her children — they were never far away when it was time to eat. The last to come was their ten year old son, Yougga, who came limping back from the potter's house, where he was sometimes allowed to help a little. One of the boy's legs was much

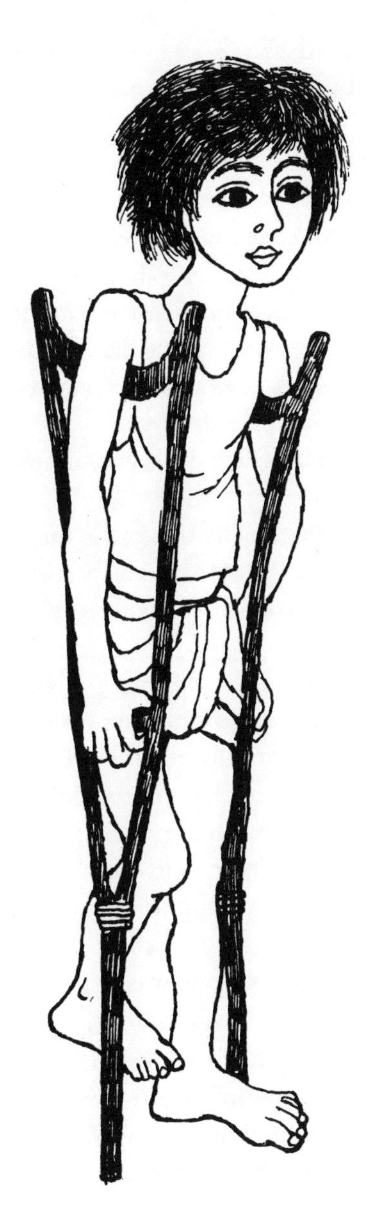

Ten-year-old Yougga came limping back from the potter's house.

too short and his foot dangled in the air. He couldn't support himself on it at all, but his father had made him a pair of crutches.

Nirad had always felt a certain sympathy for this boy, who was even more crippled than he was himself. Soon all the tanner's family had gathered together round the cooking pot which stood over a roaring hearth; the woman handed out the food. It was almost dark now. All along the street small oil lamps were being lit on the narrow covered forecourts of the houses and not far away a couple of men began to sing and play the drum.

Nirad didn't manage to light his fire; he felt very much alone.

It was festival time in the village. The rich cattle merchant who lived over in "Sudra" street was celebrating the marriage of his eldest son and all the village was taking part in the festivities.

If the parents of the bridegroom are the hosts at the wedding, it is still the father of the bride who pays for the celebrations and it is of great importance for the bride's standing in the eyes of her in-laws that the wedding should be as glittering and as sumptuous as possible. It is a costly affair for a Hindu peasant to marry off his daughter — so costly that a man with several daughters runs the risk of being ruined.

On the day in question, however, no one was thinking of considerations of that kind. It was almost evening and at the cattle merchant's house they had been celebrating throughout the day — now the wedding procession was making its way through the town. Everyone rushed to see it. Flutes, stringed instruments and drums resounded

First came the musicians.

from "Sudra" street. First came the musicians — eight men in beautiful red uniforms. Then came the female guests in their magnificent colourful saris; the wife of the cattle merchant in a deep red sari of pure Benares silk decorated with gold thread. The wife of the money-lender was dressed in a blue sari embroidered with large silver flowers — there were green saris, pink saris, yellow saris and multi-coloured saris. The women walked erect in their flowing robes, their bracelets and necklaces sparkling in the setting sun. What splendour! The spectators gasped in admiration. In the very front row came the young bride, festooned with flowers, her complexion clear. How beautiful she was! Pearls had been fastened in an arc over each of her dark eyebrows and a deep red band in the parting of her dark hair showed that she was now a married woman.

Then came the young girls, dressed no less colourfully, their long thick plaits falling to the middle of their backs — doubtless they were all thinking that it would soon be their turn to be the centre of such splendid festivities.

A group of men in magnificent green coats carried lanterns of every colour on the end of long poles. Like the musicians, they had been hired from the neighbouring town. No expense had been spared. The male guests were nearly all wearing white dhotis and loose white shirts. Only a few of the very young men were dressed in European clothes. At last came a crowd of children scattering flowers among the onlookers.

The procession made its way through all the streets — even the backstreets where the outcastes lived — and round the pool where Kengamma stood, half-hidden in the shade of the tree; the children threw grains of coloured rice and flowers over her statue. Yougga, the young son of the tanner, hobbled on his crutches beside the procession, enraptured — what pageantry! What wonderful music!

Nirad, too, was there! Whenever there were festivities in the village — music, a procession, free food — he was sure to be in the front row. The procession turned into the square and formed a semi-circle outside the temple. The bride and groom and their families went in. The others sat down outside, the Brahmins together, the Sudras together, the potters formed one group, the weavers another and the outcastes a third. No law prescribed it any longer but it was customary and they felt more at ease like that. The Brahmin priest pulled on the rope and the bells of the temple began to ring out. His

The bride and groom.

assistant blew on the horn and a passage of Holy Scripture was read aloud. At intervals the whole assembly sang hymns together. The sun had set and a long string of oil lamps were lit on the wall of the temple. From each side of the temple door shone a cluster of different coloured lamps.

It was then that the best part of the festival began. Green leaves were distributed to everyone and young girls went round with large bowls of spiced rice; everyone could eat as much as they wanted. Other girls came round with bananas, juicy mangoes and sweet dates, and the bride and groom, festooned with heavy garlands of flowers went from one person to the next, talking to everyone. Nirad felt happy and relaxed with the tanner's family. The music started up again, and now a group of young girls began to dance. How the bright saris swayed as the girls moved in a circle with small rhythmic steps to the exciting beat of the drums and the shrill sound of the flutes. Nirad's eyes shone. He was enjoying the happy atmosphere in the temple square.

The tanner began to confide quietly in Nirad, to grumble as he usually did, about the drought of the previous year which had put him in arrears with his taxes and his rates. He was always short of money, poor man, and this time it really looked serious.

"I can't see any solution, Nirad," he complained, "my debts to the money-lender run to forty-five Rupees and I only borrowed twenty from him — it's his cursed interest and now it's more than a week since I've had the smallest animal to skin, even a dog! Last time a cow died, Gopar pinched it from me. And he only has two children

— me, I have six. What is more, I have tax debts. The tax collector says that I owe him twenty Rupees on top of the twenty-five for the rent which I didn't pay this autumn — you know yourself what a mess we were all in after that terrible drought. I haven't a penny at home and our store of rice is almost exhausted — I just don't know what I shall do if you won't help me, dear brother!"

Nirad shook his head. "I am poor. You know that, yourself." Nirad had enough difficulty looking after himself; that someone might look to him for help had never even occurred to him.

"They are threatening to take our goat away! They want to put us out on the street, Nirad! I am a wretched man, tormented by the gods and abandoned by the good spirits. What must I have done in my former life to be so severely punished now?"

Nirad turned away. It was so upsetting to listen to the complaints of this unhappy man. As if he didn't have enough of his own problems. He had felt so alone since the death of his mother. What is more, they despised him in the village because he wouldn't kill himself working for a pittance for some planter, and the roof of his house was about to fall around his ears. He really had enough of his own troubles. But tonight was a celebration. Rice and bananas were freely available. Music resounded in the temple square. Girls were dancing and lights glowed behind the coloured glass of the high lamps. Drums and flutes raised the spirits and warmed the heart. No, really he didn't want to ruin such an evening by listening to the poor tanner who was constantly hounded by misfortune.

Nirad got up and slipped quietly over to where the

girls were dancing. Then someone caught him by the arm. He turned round to find that it was his neighbour from the other side of the courtyard, a skilful potter who not only made clay jugs and bowls for domestic use but also knew how to model small statues of the gods, Siva and Kali and the little elephant god, Ganesh. He painted them and sold them at the market in the neighbouring town; he was greatly respected and his house in the potters' street was white-washed and well maintained.

"Listen to me, Nirad, dear brother," he said, "there is something I have been wanting to discuss with you for some time."

"What's that?" asked Nirad, astonished. The potter had called him "brother" despite the fact that he didn't usually take any notice of his poor, lazy neighbour.

"Well, you see, I am extending my workshop. I need to build a new furnace and I haven't room in my courtyard. Now you're alone, you're a bachelor and you are probably not thinking of finding a wife. What do you want with a whole house to yourself? You're having difficulty keeping it up. Our courtyards adjoin. What would you say to the idea of selling your house to me?"

Nirad was not, like the majority of the other inhabitants of this poor street, a tenant of some rich farmer; his father had left him the little house. Nirad was dumbfounded. Sell his house! Where was he to live then?

It was as if the potter had read his thoughts.

"You could live with me. You would only have to make yourself a room in the goat's shed. It's big enough for you. You could live there for nothing on condition that you helped me once a week to fetch the potter's clay from the river."

Nirad's head was spinning. It had never occurred to him that anyone would buy his house — he had never thought that anything in his daily life could change.

"Oh - - well!" he stammered, without knowing what to answer.

"I'm offering you 300 Rupees for the old hovel," the potter went on, "and on top of that I'll sort out the goat's shed for you. You're not too keen on repairing your house — I've noticed that. When the monsoon comes your house will be as wet inside as out." Nirad took no notice of the criticism. 300 Rupees. His mind was in a turmoil. He could not grasp it.

The potter, seeing Nirad's confusion, concluded: "Think about my offer, dear brother. It stands for three days and I'll pay you in cash. I want your answer in three days." With these words the potter went on his way.

The celebrations had almost finished. The guests were leaving to go back to the cattle merchant's house where the festivities would continue, and the musicians and the dancing girls followed on behind.

A few young men remained seated in the warmth of the night and played the drums and sang but the older people made their way home and parents made sure that their daughters accompanied them dutifully.

Nirad took himself off home too, despite the fact that he was usually an enthusiastic drummer and singer. Tonight he was so bewildered that he had only one aim in mind — to go home and think in peace about the potter's staggering proposition. He sat down in the darkness on his little terrace, huddled up with his tattered blanket over his shoulders. There was no question of falling asleep yet.

On the neighbouring terrace the tanner and his wife were also sitting in the darkness. The children were already asleep. Their parents sat and talked together softly in tired, disheartened voices.

Nirad thought about what he could do with all that money if he did decide to sell his house. He could buy paint for his boat which leaked and was badly in need of repair. He could rig it with a small sail — he had been

Nirad thought about what he could do with all that money.

dreaming of that for a long time. He could buy himself some cotton material for a loin-cloth — several loin-cloths and a shining copper cup to drink out of; his mother had dreamed of such a cup but she had never had one. A new cover wouldn't be a bad idea either, a white woollen blanket with a red border like those that Kara, the weaver made for the best families in the village! But people would point at him if he decked himself out like that, he, who belonged to the tanners' caste, to the untouchables. For, even if according to the law there was no longer such a thing as an untouchable, things had not changed that much in the village. People belonging to higher castes would always wave him out of the way when they met him in the street so that his shadow would not fall on them, and he for his part would take his place in the gutter unhesitatingly. So what would he do with a white blanket with red braid? He would make himself ridiculous, that was all.

Then he heard the woman next door sobbing.

"The goat," she wailed, "if he takes the goat, as he threatened, we shall die of starvation. What can we do? If only the boys could earn a little, but there is no work here."

"If only the village were a little bigger and everyone didn't know each other we could have made a little profit out of Yougga," the tanner answered quietly. "He could have sat outside the temple and begged like Koum, the blind man. In larger towns a cripple like Yougga can easily earn enough for his food and more by begging; but it wouldn't work here where everyone knows us; no-one would give him anything."

"You're right," said his wife despondently, "but what can we do?"

"You remember," rejoined the tanner, "after the terrible drought eight years ago when many of the poor were starving to death and many of the young people left their homes, there were people who sold their children to travelling beggars?"

"Yes, one of my uncles sold his son, the one that was born with only one hand, to a man like that who bought children — but you still can't be thinking of selling Yougga!" The woman's voice was indignant.

"They used to pay 100 Rupees for a child capable of begging," continued the tanner, after a moment's thought. "100 Rupees! and they say that a good beggar can earn more in a day than a coolie or a farm labourer! Otherwise the travelling beggars wouldn't pay so much."

"Now, I warn you here and now," said the woman, shocked, "if you sell our poor little Yougga to a stranger, I shall go straight back to my parents and you can manage all on your own!"

"And what about the other children? No, no, you stay where you are," said the tanner. "I didn't say that I was going to sell him. What's more there haven't been any buyers about for a long time. Don't get so excited."

A little while later the potter added softly: "But it won't be easy for the boy to make his way in life."

"He could learn to mend shoes and sew sandals," suggested his wife. "Perhaps Nirad could teach him."

"That lazybones, Nirad! There's a fine teacher for you! Let's go to bed, I am very tired, I have a headache and it's late." Nirad started when he heard what was being said about him. And yet it was he, the poor, lazy shoemaker's son who was suddenly going to become a man of means, while the wretched tanner's family became more and more deeply entrenched in their poverty. No doubt it was their "karma". The gods had so determined it, but all the same it was strange and he felt sorry for the poor wretches, particularly for Yougga with his deformed leg.

But charity must begin at home and lending money to the tanner was like throwing it in the river; he could be sure of never seeing it again. No! he must think of himself, of how best to use all that money. Rent some land? Buy an ox and cart? No, the life of a peasant was hard and uncertain and without a wife it was altogether impossible. No, no, that was not for him. But then what was he to do with all that money? Exhausted, at last he fell asleep.

2 *Nirad Has An Idea*

Two days later they came to take away the tanner's goat. The tanner himself was lying in bed with a fever — from time to time he suffered from attacks of malaria — when the moneylender's representative arrived.

"I am to greet you on behalf of my master," said the unfortunate messenger, "and tell you that if you don't give me 30 Rupees, I am to seize your goat — this is the third time that I have had to come here."

The woman cried, her husband groaned feverishly, and the children stared in terror at this wicked man who calmly untied the goat from its stake and led it away down the narrow street. The other women came out of

Two days later they came to take away the tanner's goat.

their houses; they abused and threatened this hated man, for most of them knew him from personal experience.

"Your master is a real bloodsucker," they shouted. "He's the devil in person. He'll be punished in his next life. He'll be a goat himself! Or a snake! A worm to be trodden on! Tell him that if you dare! You devil's accomplice, you!"

But what good did all that do? The servant was used to such abuse. It went hand in hand with his job. The goat belonged to the money-lender because the tanner had never paid his dues. The law was on the side of the money-lender and wasn't the law there to be adhered to? Who cared about a poor tanner and his family who would go hungry?

The neighbouring women went back to their chores. They washed the linen, went to fetch water, ground the grains of corn and maize and kneaded dough to make bread, they looked after their children and sewed their clothes; there was quite enough to do and each one had quite enough worries of her own. Everyone in this street was poor and nearly everyone owed money to the money-lender. The tanner would just have to sort out his own problems like everyone else in this world; no doubt it was his karma — punishment for evil which he had committed in his previous existence. There was no escaping the will of the gods! Everyone must put up with his destiny.

When Nirad came back from fishing that night with a modest catch of two small fishes, he saw the tanner's wife squatting under the roof of the terrace beside the mat on which her husband was sleeping feverishly.

"They have taken the goat," reported Yougga. He looked very pale and upset.

Nirad was quite overcome.

"You can take my fish for supper," he said generously and held them out over the dividing wall.

The woman, numb with grief, didn't seem to notice anything but Yougga beamed with delight as he took them.

"The gods will reward you," he said.

A moment later Nirad regretted his generosity. It was easier to cook fish than to knead the dough for chapatis. Still, that was too bad. After all there was merit to be earned by helping those less fortunate than oneself; what's more, he had more important considerations to think about than whether he would have fish or chapatis for his supper. The poor shoe-maker's son was in the throes of getting used to the prospect of being a man with money, lots of money. His horizons were broadening. New possibilities were revealing themselves. Nirad had always been a dreamer. That was perhaps why until now he had not risen to anything greater than being the son of a hard-working shoe-maker. A strange thought had come to him today as he was sitting in his boat on the river in a creek full of junks. He was looking at the brown water of the river which flowed gently towards the far distant south when he felt a strange compulsion to follow the flow of the water. It crossed his mind that far away in the south this small river flowed into the Ganges. What if he, poor Nirad, were to go on a pilgrimage to Benares! The rich money-lender had been to Benares several times, so too had some of the Brahmins and some of the richer Sudras, but he had never heard of an outcaste who had been on pilgrimage. To travel to Benares, to bathe in the sacred Ganges and so to be cleansed of all sin was an important achievement and one which earned favour in the eyes of the gods. Nirad's heart filled with a strange and impatient yearning at the very thought of it. That would really be living!

No sooner had the idea come to him that it blossomed forth like a bright flower from its green bud; of course, he would go by boat. The river which flowed past the village was a tributary of a larger river which emptied itself into the Ganges. In his small boat, he could row or sail as far as the holy city of Benares with its many temples and its wide steps which led down to the water's edge. Pilgrims and holy men gathered there to bathe in the Ganges and to greet the rising sun with prayers and hymns. Nirad would see it all for himself if he sold his little house, where he led a poor, lonely existence in the street of the outcastes. Here, in the village, he would never be anything but the lazy son of a shoe-maker, Nirad with the limp, but out there great things and marvellous adventures awaited him. Nirad was so absorbed in his dreams that he completely forgot the poor tanner's family in the house next door.

On the following day he went to see the potter whose courtyard adjoined Nirad's vegetable garden. The potter's house was built like all the better houses in the village, with a clay wall round its courtyard. Inside this wall were the workshop and the house itself which contained several rooms; everything was well maintained and white-washed.

Nirad remained standing in the middle of the courtyard as a mark of respect.

On his terrace, in front of the house, the potter was in the process of painting little clay statuettes of the gods; he was a real artist and his small religious statues were in great demand at the market in the large neighbouring town. Nirad remained standing in the middle of the courtyard in front of the house, as a mark of respect. As a former outcaste he did not dare to draw any closer. The customs of bygone days forbad it.

"Well, my brother Nirad," cried the potter, "have you decided to sell? Your time will soon have run out and I have the money all ready to give to you."

"It's agreed. I'll sell you my house," said Nirad, with a trembling voice. It had been a difficult decision for him to make. "Just as I thought, you're a sensible man," said the potter, pleased; now he could extend his workshop and take on another assistant. "And you, do you want to move into the goat's shed?"

"No," said Nirad — he was so moved he could hardly speak. "I am going on a pilgrimage to Benares."

For a moment there was a stupefied silence. The potter's wife, who was in the middle of grinding corn in a stone mill, stopped and stared at him in astonishment. A poor pariah wanting to go on pilgrimage! Even her husband would never have dreamed of that.

"To Benares!" There was a mixture of admiration and resentment in the potter's voice. "Of course, you can spend your money however you wish. But wouldn't it be wiser to invest all that money in a plot of land. You could plant a few coconut palms on it, grow vegetables. You could look after it yourself and it would give you enough to live on together with a little shoemaking. Now you have the opportunity to be independent with a comfortable livelihood."

"Independence at the price of hard work," thought Nirad. He would have the tax-collector and the moneylender on his back in no time. No, he had taken it into his head to set out to see the world. He wanted to go to Benares, the holy city and bathe in the waters of the Ganges. Nirad shook his head.

"Alright then, if you're so clever, you do as you think best," said the potter. "If you want to throw your money out of the window like that, by the end of the year you will be as poor as you used to be, but that's your business. There's the money!" He took out a linen bag and shook it. It was full and chinked as it was shaken; Nirad's heart beat loudly.

The potter came out into the courtyard and dropped the purse into Nirad's outstretched hands — how heavy it was! And all those chinking coins were his! "Be sensible with your money," advised the potter. "Don't go telling everyone that you're walking about with all that cash on you. Hide the purse well under your loincloth. You must realise that there are not only saints and devout pilgrims on the streets of Benares. There are also thieves, imposters and grasping tradesmen — so I'm told."

Nirad was certain that no-one would cheat him. After all he hadn't been born yesterday. He bowed deeply to the potter and retreated, walking backwards.

"When are you leaving? When can I take possession of the house? A lawyer will have to draw up the bill of sale, but I'll see to that."

"I shall leave as soon as I am ready."

"And your furnishings — are you taking them? I don't suppose they amount to much."

No, there was nothing very much, thought Nirad. A cooking pot, an iron stove and a few water jugs, bowls and some small tools. And he couldn't take his mat with him. He would give it to the tanner who could make good use of it, he thought as he walked home.

The tanner's family! Those poor people had always been good neighbours. What a shame that everything was turning out so badly for them. Of course they were not the only people in the village who were suffering.

Hunger was reflected in many people's eyes for the awful drought of the previous year had driven many into the arms of the money-lender and once within his grasp, it was almost impossible to break free because of the excessive interest which continued to accumulate. No, it was not easy to be poor, particularly with a horde of children to feed. He, Nirad, was lucky to be independent and free to do whatever he liked.

He could give the tanner some money or buy his goat back for him but in doing so he would only win him a brief respite. In two months' time they would be back to square one. Anyway he needed the money himself for his long journey. He needed one or two things now; he would have to buy food en route and he would still have to live while he was in Benares. That was without thinking any further ahead; Nirad didn't want to look that far. One step at a time!

The tanner was gradually recovering from his attack of fever. He was sitting on his bed looking pale and weak. His wife was in the middle of cooking rice for their supper. They had one sack of rice left to eat and some vegetables in the garden. But what would happen when the rice ran out? Then there was the tax collector who might arrive any day. Would they be turned out of their house? Nirad leaned over the dividing wall: "I have sold my house!" he announced and the poor, disheartened people looked at him as if he had gone mad.

"What have you done?" asked the man, agitated.

"I have sold my house to the potter. I'm going on pilgrimage to Benares."

The neighbours gaped. The news almost made them

forget their own need.

"When?" stammered the tanner.

"Over the next few days. I only want to buy a few small things — a new loin-cloth, a shirt, a cover and a sail for the boat."

"You're going by boat?"

"But of course. When one has a boat, it's the most sensible means of transport."

"It will be a long journey, Nirad."

"That doesn't matter."

The tanner had instantly realised that Nirad now had money, lots of money.

"My dear brother Nirad," he began to whine but Nirad beat a hasty retreat. He knew that the tanner was about to ask him for money and he hadn't yet really decided what answer he would give him. He went into the courtyard at the back of the house to collect up the tools and things that he thought he would need for the journey.

When darkness began to fall, he came back to light the fire and make himself some chapatis. Just then he saw a little misshapen shadow in a corner of his terrace. Two crutches protruded from it. It was Yougga.

"Is it true that you are leaving for Benares?" whispered the boy, his eyes shining.

"Yes, as true as I am standing here now."

"Nirad, take me with you," implored Yougga, eagerly. "Take me! I can beg for you. I can help you by getting food."

"Do you know how to beg?"

"Yes, I've even heard my father say that in another

town, where nobody knew me, I could earn a lot of money because I'm a cripple."

Nirad knew that it was true and suddenly it occurred to him that it would be nice to have some company on the long journey. Yougga was a good, capable boy and it would be better to go as a pair than all alone. Furthermore it was true that the boy could beg a little money for them both as they made their way to Benares. Perhaps the boy could even bring him in a little profit.

"Yes, but what would your parents say?"

"I don't know but there are so many of us in the house and it's hard enough to feed us all. Now they've taken the goat," the boy's voice trembled.

Nirad thought about it. There was no doubt about it, it would not be a bad idea to have this boy with him on his journey.

"Can't you ask them?" pleaded Yougga.

He had always been fond of Nirad who took him out in his boat from time to time and let him fish. A journey down the river in Nirad's boat was an exciting prospect for the little lame boy who had little hope of a rosy future in the village where he was born.

Nirad promised to think about it and Yougga limped off into the darkness.

The following morning, Nirad knew that he wanted to have Yougga with him on his adventure and he was also certain that the boy could earn more than his upkeep in the places where they stopped en route.

The tanner was on his feet again and working in his little garden.

"Good day, dear brother," said Nirad politely.

"Good day, brother Nirad," replied the tanner with alacrity, coming towards him. "I just wanted to ask you something." Nirad interrupted him quickly. "I wanted to ask you something too, dear neighbour. Could you give your son, Yougga, permission to come with me on pilgrimage to Benares?"

The tanner stared at him in astonishment. "Yougga, what can you do with him?"

"He's a good boy and I like him. It wouldn't be much fun to embark on such a journey alone. And in any case, he could beg a little money for us both," he added hesitatingly.

The tanner seized on the idea instantly. "Yes, beg! That's what I've always said. With his crooked, useless leg that boy could earn a lot of money, if only he were to beg in a town where nobody knew him. He could make you rich, Nirad."

"I don't know about that, but I've no doubt he could earn enough to provide for his own needs."

"Far more! I think you could live off what he'd bring in, brother Nirad. Why else do you think people buy children like him for good money and take them into the big cities?"

Nirad realised that he would have to bargain.

"How much are you thinking of asking for the loan of your son for my journey?"

"Loan? When do you think you're going to get back then? It will be relatively easy for you to sail to Benares with the current behind you, but coming back, you'll have the current against you and that will be much more difficult. Anyway you can earn your living much

"What are you up to?" asked the tanner's wife suspiciously.

more easily there as a stranger, particularly with the boy. He could be worth his weight in gold. No, if you want to take my son with you, you will have to buy him. Give me 130 Rupees and you've got a bargain."

"130 Rupees! 50 would be more than enough!"

"Are you out of your mind? My wife's brother sold one of their children to a travelling beggar eight years ago — it was during that terrible famine, you remember, and he was given 100 Rupees cash!"

His wife came over to them. "What are you up to?" she asked suspiciously.

"Nirad wants to know if he can take Yougga with him on his long journey," answered the tanner.

"You really want to take the boy with you?" The woman was astonished.

"Yes, he can beg for them both," explained the tanner. "It's quite an advantage to have a little bandy-legged boy with you."

"But what does Yougga say to all this?" said the boy's mother anxiously.

"Yougga is very keen to come with me," said Nirad. "He came to ask me himself."

The mother went off to look for her son. She wanted to talk to him herself. He must not be sent away against his will.

The tanner and Nirad bargained for a while before settling on the price of 100 Rupees, in exchange for which he would belong to Nirad as if he were his own son.

What an uproar there was in the untouchables' street and indeed throughout the village, when the news spread that the tanner had sold his crippled son, Yougga, to Nirad.

"How could the tanner do such a thing as to sell his own child to that good-for-nothing!" said some. Others thought that they would make a fine pair of vagabonds to send on pilgrimage to Benares.

That shoe-maker's son certainly had a nerve! No doubt the money had gone to his head.

There were those too who secretly envied Nirad and Yougga, two lucky lads, who could set off as free as the wind on such a fantastic journey, but then what would become of them when the money ran out — as it was bound to sooner or later! All the sensible people shook their heads.

Nevertheless, Yougga was extremely happy and the

tanner and his wife could not help but be pleased to have solved their financial problems in such an unexpected way, even if they weren't altogether happy at the thought of what could happen to their son far away in an unfamiliar world. Nirad was a kindly sort of man who would certainly never harm their son but he was also a lazy good-for-nothing, incapable of holding down a proper job. After all, the people out there must be different and live differently. Yet the gods must have had a role to play in it, for this was the answer to the most fervent prayers of the tanner's family.

The tanner sat down to reckon up. First he would buy back the goat. What a joy for the whole family! Then he would have to pay his outstanding taxes to get rid of that importunate tax-collector. He would have to pay the rent too. There might even be enough to pay off an instalment to the money-lender, but he also needed to buy some material to make saris for his wife and his eldest daughters together with a new loin-cloth for himself! Yes, there was no shortage of things on which to spend money. Furthermore there was always the chance that the priest would kill his old donkey and he had promised the work to the poor tanner. It was as if fortune was smiling on him at last!

When Nirad counted out 100 Rupees and handed them to the tanner it was a significant moment for the whole family but it was Yougga who was most proud, for it was thanks to him and his crooked leg that all this had come about.

3 *The Journey Begins*

The boat had been repaired, repainted and equipped with a small sail. Some jars of flour and rice were stowed on board together with Nirad's bundle containing a change of loin-cloth, a shirt and an old coat which the potter had given him. Yougga's mother had sewn a strong linen bag for the boy to sling over his shoulder like a real begging bag. She had also given him a small tin bowl like the ones beggars usually used to collect their money, which would serve him for eating and drinking too. An old pullover for cold nights and a tattered woollen blanket in which he could wrap himself completed his equipment.

On the day of their departure, all the tanner's family and a number of curious people from the street accompanied Nirad and Yougga to the riverbank. Some had brought small presents: green coconuts, two or three bananas, a small bag of roasted peanuts. It was a major event for these poor people and it was the first time in living memory that someone from the outcastes' street had left to go on pilgrimage to Benares. Would they ever see the two pilgrims again? Yougga's mother asked her son to bring her back a jug of holy water from the Ganges if ever he came home again. Only the Brahmin priest had ever done such a thing and it had made him very famous. The pride of the tanner and his wife at the thought that their son was embarking on this fantastic journey was not without foundation.

It was a little after sunrise. The sky was still red and the

All the tanner's family accompanied Nirad and Yougga to the riverbank.

air was deliciously fresh. The low sun was reflected in the tranquil waters of the river and shone on myriad droplets scattered over the grass and the reeds. Yougga clambered on board on all fours and his father handed him his crutches. The thin boy stood on one leg and propped his other knee on the thwart. In that way he hoped to be able to scull the boat with one oar. Nirad jumped aboard and seized the other one. The net and the other bits of fishing gear were carefully arranged in the bow. Nirad pulled himself up straight and stole a glance at the riverbank. It was an important moment: for the first time ever the poor, bandy-legged shoe-maker's son was the focal point of everybody's interest. People were waving. Yougga's mother burst into tears. His father shouted goodbye at the top of his voice and called upon the gods to bless the two courageous travellers. "May the good spirits watch over you, my son," he cried. "I will offer up a chicken for you at the altar of Kengamma."

Yougga waved goodbye with a lump in his throat. Would he ever see his father and mother and all his brothers and sisters again? And the old grey goat which they had triumphantly fetched back from the money-lender yesterday? At that moment he felt very small and frightened. The people over on the riverbank already seemed minute and the straw roofs of the village were disappearing beyond the tops of the palm trees. Now large junks concealed the last view of the familiar

riverbank, his family and his friends. They were off on their hazardous journey to the sacred river, to the Ganges, to Benares!

The adventure had begun.

All day long they sculled their boat, rowed or drifted round the bends in the little river but they were still on familiar ground. Nirad had often ventured into these parts.

It was very sultry. The hot season was approaching, spring was giving way to summer and the dryness was beginning to make itself felt. The river was very narrow in places. The water flowed between wide mud banks and here and there large islands of yellowish-brown silt blocked their passage, but the small boat with its flat bottom always found a way past.

There was no wind but the current carried the boat along fast enough. Nirad set up his fishing line, baited it and cast it over the stern. He and Yougga had nothing to do but steer the boat clear of the mud and the rushes with the oars, and wait for a bite. It was a very pleasant way of passing the time.

When the sun was high in the sky, casting its burning rays on the little river, Nirad had the idea of fixing the sail over the front of the boat. Then he stretched out for an afternoon nap in the shade, having directed Yougga to steer the boat clear of the mudbanks, without forgetting to keep an eye on the line. Yougga was proud of the trust vested in him and Nirad, delighted to have so eager a helper on the journey, made himself comfortable on his blanket and soon dozed off.

"What if there are crocodiles about?" wondered Yougga with a shudder. At home, in the village, people had said that there were crocodiles in this part of the river, but no one had actually seen one in recent years. People hunted crocodiles because their skin was very valuable.

In the larger rivers, particularly in the Ganges, there were still crocodiles among the tall rushes — so Nirad had told him. Yougga kept his eyes wide open. There were so many things to look at: pink flamingoes strutted on the dry clayey banks and there were many other waders that he didn't recognise. A family of ducks and ducklings passed by — a group of vultures wheeled and circled over a small island. No doubt some dead animal had been stranded there.

The intensity of the sun made his head swim. Nirad was lucky to be lying in the shade but then it occurred to Yougga that he could put his blanket over his head. That would give him some protection from the burning rays.

From time to time he pulled in the fishing line to see whether a fish had taken the bait, but there was nothing there. In the fields beyond the high banks he could see people working. They were rushing to drain the valuable water via small channels and ditches into the rice fields. It would soon be time to harvest the rice and pick the sugar cane, which would later be loaded in large bundles onto the backs of camels or donkeys. Yougga longed to bite into a juicy sugar cane; surely that evening, when it was dark, he would be able to sneak into a field and grab a couple of canes.

At last he had a fish on the line. He pulled it in eagerly, took it off the hook and threw it into the bottom of the boat, where there was a little water under the slats. It lay there with its tail thrashing, gasping for breath.

"Nirad!" he cried proudly. "I've caught a fish!" Nirad woke at last, refreshed by his long snooze. "Good," he said, looking around him. "Just one more like it and that's dinner sorted out. Give me the line and I'll see to it."

"I'm tired of the sun," complained Yougga.

"Crawl into the shade. I'll take over the rest now," said Nirad. "It's no longer quite so hot. I think I shall row for a while to speed us up because we must reach a bend in the river with large banyan trees on it before we moor for the night."

They changed places. Yougga crept under the sail to sleep and Nirad took charge of the boat.

At sunset they reached a bend in the river covered with large trees.

"We're going to stop here," said Nirad. "I have to tell you that this is a holy place. A hermit lives here. He is very devout, that is if he's actually here — sometimes he goes off on long journeys to beg, but the people in the surrounding neighbourhood prefer him to stay in this small wood and bring him food so that they can ask him for help. He talks to them, advises them and gives them his blessing."

Yougga looked excitedly at the small dark wood of ancient banyan trees. Underneath the lofty treetops grew a confusing mass of long tuberous roots which plunged into the earth. It was like an enchanted forest.

In the shelter of the bend they found a quiet creek and it was there that they went ashore.

"First collect a little dry grass and some twigs so that we can cook the fish, and then afterwards we will go and see if the hermit is there; he has a small temple, underneath a large tree. I would like him to bless us. It would bode well for our journey."

Yougga collected the wood and soon a little fire was burning under the cooking pot. Some boys from the neighbouring village appeared on the embankment and came to stare curiously at the two strangers.

"Is the hermit in his temple?" Nirad asked them. "Or is he away?"

"He's here," nodded the boys. "He's there in the wood. Where are you going?"

"We are pilgrims en route for Benares," announced Nirad with great dignity.

The boys gaped in admiration.

Nirad and Yougga ate some rice with their fish. By this time it was pitch dark. Nirad extinguished the last glowing embers and stood up.

"Come on, we're going to see the hermit."

Yougga followed him into the shadowy banyan wood; in the darkness it was not always easy for him to climb over the twisted roots with his crutches but soon they saw a glimmer of light between the sinuous trunks. The holy man was sitting in the very midst of them, wearing the saffron robes of a monk. His hair was long and tangled. Before him burned a candle. A picture of Siva was propped against the trunk of the tree and the face of the god seemed extraordinarily lifelike in the dim flickering light. A wreath of flowers adorned the sacred image and before it was a bowl half full of rice.

Nirad stooped to kiss the hermit's naked foot and Yougga followed suit. Looking up, his gaze met that of the holy man. His eyes were bright and shining and it was as if they looked right into the soul.

Nirad poured a little rice from his bag into the bowl for

The holy man was sitting in the very midst of the sinuous trunks.

in that way the rice which he kept would be blessed by the god. "Oh holy Saddhu," he murmured. "We are two repentant pilgrims en route for Benares, will you bless us?"

The holy man looked at the two poor creatures in astonishment. "It is truly a formidable mission that you have undertaken," he said. Do you know that there are many weeks of travelling ahead before you reach that city? You must cross jungles, marshes, mountains and rivers, for I imagine that you do not have the means to take the train that breathes fire?"

"We are travelling by boat, holy Father," replied Nirad with certain self-satisfaction.

"And the boy there is your son?"

"He is my adopted son."

Yougga saw that the old man had three grey lines painted in ash across his forehead. His bare arms were tattooed.

Nirad took out a Rupee from the pocket under his loin-cloth and let it fall with a clatter into the hermit's begging bowl, because there is merit to be earned by giving alms to a holy man.

The hermit dipped the tip of his finger into a little bowl of red dye. Nirad and Yougga knelt before him and he imprinted a red mark on their foreheads between their eyebrows.

"A blessing on your expedition," he said. "May the gods be good to you and may you achieve the goal that you have set yourself."

Then he turned his head away and his expression became distant.

Nirad and Yougga got up and picked their way between the twisted trees back to the river, now bathed in the pale light of the half-moon.

"He is a very holy man," whispered Yougga, impressed.

"Yes, very," said Nirad. "They say that he performs miracles."

They found the boat and curled up in the bottom of it, each wrapped in his blanket for the nights were cold on the river.

The first day of their journey was over.

4 *Yougga Tries To Beg*

"There must be a large town up there," said Nirad one fine day, "because there are wide steps leading down to the river and two large boats are moored there."

They had passed out of the familiar little stream into a bigger, wider river carrying much more water. Now for the first time they saw a ghat, a mooring place where steps came down to the water's edge. In India there are no quays and jetties for mooring along the riverbank as there are in our country, because they would be flooded and destroyed at high water; instead there are flights of steps.

Yougga looked with interest in the direction of the town. There were women doing their washing on the riverbank and children playing beside the water.

"Here, you can try your hand at begging," suggested Nirad.

Yougga was seized with panic.

"Go on into the town until you find the temple," explained Nirad. "Stand there and, above all, remember to look pathetic. Look, you can take my old loin-cloth which is dirty and tattered. If you can look a bit more hunchbacked all the better. Have a go!"

Nirad practised with the boy until he had learnt to look really pitiful.

"What am I to say?" asked the boy, with his heart in his mouth.

"Do you remember what old Koum used to say in the village? And the old leper who had no fingers or toes any more? Didn't it go something like: 'Oh devout and good hearted pilgrims, have pity on me poor wretched worm that I am and earn eternal merit in the eyes of the gods by giving alms to a poor crippled orphan child.' Remember you're a crippled child and not a blind old man like Koum."

Yougga repeated the words as best he could.

"You say it in such a ridiculous way that no-one will ever believe you. You must look as if you are on the brink of tears and moan. Don't you remember old Koum?"

Yougga tried to put a little more feeling into what he was saying.

"That was a bit better," conceded Nirad. "But now listen to me. Oh you devout and good hearted visitors to the temple, you devout and good hearted pilgrims!" he cried in a tearful voice. "Have pity on me, wretched creature that I am. Earn eternal merit in the eyes of the gods by giving of your charity to a small starving crippled child who is reaching out his hand to you—just one small coin from your abundance and the gods will reward you!"

In the end Nirad was reasonably satisfied and Yougga was set down at the foot of the steps.

He climbed up on all fours wearing the dirty ragged loin-cloth, his begging bag over his shoulder and his bowl strung on a cord round his neck. He was very concerned as to how his efforts would work out. When he next saw Nirad would he have a few coins? Many perhaps? He was going to have to learn somehow for this was going to be his means of earning a living for several years, perhaps even for the rest of his life. Yougga shuddered, wondering if it was difficult to become a beggar. In the meantime Nirad had said that he would try and fish.

At the top of the steps beyond the embankment Yougga saw a dusty path leading to quite a large village made up of huts built out of dried mud. Further on, in the main street there were brick houses, and some were even white-washed and looked very attractive.

Soon he reached the market place where many tradesmen offered their wares and there too, stood the temple. He hobbled on his crutches up to the door of the temple. On either side of it were stalls with garlands of flowers, images of the gods, sticks of incense, oil lamps and a multitude of other things for sale.

He stood himself there, looking as pitiful and hunchbacked as possible, slouched over his crutches. With a trembling hand he held out his begging bowl but just then an old woman arrived and in her fury, delivered such a blow to one of Yougga's crutches that he nearly fell over. She yelled at him to disappear and a one-legged man came limping over to abuse and insult him too.

"You mangy dog," she shouted. "You miserable cur! What do you think you're doing here? Scum of the earth, little snake!"

Other beggars arrived on the scene — blind men, lepers, cripples — and all of them yelled at him, threatened him and shouted at him to clear off. If he didn't, they would crush him to pulp and break up his miserable crutches and burn them. Yougga was so frightened that he hurried away as fast as his crutches would carry him. The temple beggars continued to bawl after him.

They all yelled at him, threatened him and shouted at him to clear off

Yougga was crying with fear and apprehension as he limped away towards the market place where he tried to hide himself as quickly as possible in the crowd. So it was that difficult to get permission to beg! But how had the others been allowed to? Perhaps they had all known each other in the first place and agreed amongst themselves that they would not tolerate other beggars joining them.

Yougga was in the depths of despair. He knew that Nirad had paid a lot of money for him, in the hope that he would earn at least some of it back. If he had to go back to the boat empty-handed, Nirad would most certainly be furious. Perhaps he wouldn't want to keep him any more — and then what would become of him, and all those wonderful expressions Nirad had taught him! He would probably never need them!

Yougga looked around him, perplexed. He was now

in a very narrow bazaar street. There were all kinds of street stalls and hordes of people: goldsmiths, coppersmiths, shoemakers, potters and silk merchants. Yougga had never seen so many beautiful stalls all together in one place. Whatever else happened he was resolved to take advantage of the opportunity and look at all those beautiful things.

He hobbled cautiously down the street looking behind him as he went. No, no-one was following him any more. No-one was taking any notice of the poor boy on his crutches. He stopped in front of a baker's stall. What a tempting display of sweetmeats! The baker was in the middle of making rice cakes in an enormous cooking pot full of fat. How wonderful it smelt! Yougga paused to watch. Then he ventured to try and hold out his bowl.

"I'm so hungry," he murmured, then added more loudly: "my father and mother are dead, take pity on a poor crippled child!" And much to Yougga's surprise and delight, the kindly baker put a small cake in his begging bowl.

"The gods will reward you," murmured Yougga and hurried away as if afraid that the baker would regret his generosity.

A small thin girl in a dirty, tattered sari, carrying a baby in a cloth at her hip, was coming slowly up the street, her begging bowl held out before her, her back bent under the weight of the child she carried. There were several very small coins in her bowl. A fat woman dressed in a yellow floral patterned sari dropped in another small coin. The girl's face was tired and washed out, devoid of any expression. She looked almost old despite the fact that she was only eleven or twelve at the very most. Yougga was so distressed by the sight of her that, quite impulsively, he put half his rice cake in the girl's begging bowl. She glanced at him without smiling and continued on her way. Was that the fate of all beggar children? he wondered fearfully.

He finished his rice cake and looked about him. There were so many things to look at! Just opposite him, there was a stall full of saris of every conceivable colour — with flowers, patterns, gold embroidery. Each piece of material competed with the next for sheer brilliance. Next to it was a store with large silver rings and bracelets and long rows of pearl necklaces — what extravagance! There was also a stall with magnificent saddles for donkeys and camels and another with painted and gilded pictures of the gods. It was there that Yougga had the idea of going along the street and trying to beg like the young girl. It was easier to pass unnoticed in the bazaar and if he noticed any other beggars he would be on his guard. He hunched up his back as much as possible and moved slowly forward on his crutches, stopping from time to time to say in a plaintive voice: "Show charity towards a poor crippled child who no longer has any parents."

Most people passed by without taking any notice of him, but from time to time someone would drop a small coin into his begging bowl. Some of them threatened him and said angrily: "Go away, little toad!" or insulted him in other ways, but a little beggar boy has to learn to take that kind of thing.

He limped down one side of the road and back up the

He couldn't forget the young girl with the baby.

other. In the square he made quite sure that none of the beggars from the temple noticed him. He slipped along the foot of the wall and out of the town and it was only then that he stopped under a dusty fig tree to count his money. There were 70 Pice. That made almost one Rupee — it wasn't bad but what would Nirad say?

He climbed down the steps and sat on the bottom one until towards evening Nirad rowed over to pick him up. Yougga crawled on board.

"Well, how much have you made?" asked Nirad.

"70 Pice," replied Yougga proudly.

"That's not really very much but you'll learn with time!" Nirad tipped the money into the bag under his loin-cloth.

Yougga told him what had happened at the door of the temple.

"Alright then, you'll have to keep away from the temple, it's a shame because the people who go to the temple are the most generous, but the street vendors didn't do badly either. Practice will make perfect. Now we're going to row across to the other bank to bathe and have something to eat. We'll be better off on the other side tonight, there are so many people over here."

Nirad had not caught anything but they had enough flour left in the jar to make chapatis.

Yougga was proud, despite everything, to have earned almost a Rupee on his first day of work as a beggar.

He couldn't forget the young girl with the baby; her face had been so hard and grey, as if she had never known any joy in life, No, it was not all that easy to be a real beggar.

5 *Adversity*

By this time it was summer and the heat was heavy and oppressive. Even the wide river they had now reached was almost dry. There were large banks of sand and yellow silt on either side of them and at midday the sun shone so fiercely that, if they didn't manage to find a patch of land with a few dusty trees to provide them with a little shade, they had to slide under the sail. Most of the irrigation channels and ditches along the river were completely dry and in the fields the earth was so dry that it had cracked open. The crops were withering away. It was lucky that the rice and sugar cane had already been harvested.

The tufts of grass on the dykes and riverbanks were all yellow and faded. The dusty leaves of all the trees were shrivelled up and some had fallen to the ground. Nature seemed to lie dying; everything groaned under the overpowering heat and panted with thirst. Rain — every man, beast and plant craved for rain. If only the monsoon, with its life-giving rains would hurry up and come.

In this scorching heat Nirad fell ill. He was feverish and had pains in his stomach. He couldn't keep any food down and was suffering from a continual thirst, but there was nothing to drink apart from the tepid, muddy water of the river. Was it some sort of stomach infection? Or had he been stung by some poisonous insect? There were so many insects flying about over the river and the dried out rushes! Perhaps it was swamp-fever or malaria? In either case it would make no difference for Yougga had no medicaments to give him and he didn't know how to help the sick man. Poor Nirad remained stretched out under the sail, moaning because of the heat, and racked with pains in his head and his stomach. Yougga had to look after everything, keep the boat heading downstream and from time to time make himself something to eat. Nirad, for his part, couldn't eat anything without vomiting.

Their supply of flour was exhausted and there was hardly any rice left either.

"You must try and beg," murmured Nirad, "but to be on the safe side take one Rupee out of my purse and buy some flour, rice and tomatoes — whatever you want. You must be able to find a village where you can buy something to eat."

Yougga moved Nirad's loin-cloth to one side and found the leather purse. It was stuffed full of money. He carefully counted out one Rupee in small coins. It was easier to deal with small change. Then he set about looking for a village, keeping up the speed of the boat by rowing it and punting it.

After a while he reached a real ghat and beyond it he could make out houses, a lot of houses — it must be a proper city. He could see domes and towers. Yougga had never seen such a large town. Near the river stood an imposing palace surrounded by a great wall. For an instant Yougga forgot Nirad and all their problems to wonder at the magnificent buildings. The first ones he passed were built out of red brick surrounded by walls and lofty towers. Then he noticed a marvellous monument in white marble with domes flanked by spires.

The Taj Mahal.

Yougga had never dreamed that anything so beautiful and sumptuous existed. The person who lived there must be at least a king, possibly even an emperor.

Yougga longed to go and have a closer look at this marvel, and as there had to be a big city near a palace of that kind, he decided to go ashore. He punted his boat as far as the dusty bank at the foot of the wall and dropped anchor on a flat sand bank. Then he said to Nirad: "We've arrived at a large city. I'm going ashore here."

"Is there some water in my bowl?" asked Nirad huskily.

"I have just filled it up."

"Do you think you could bring me back a water melon?"

"I'll try," promised Yougga. Then he went hobbling off on his crutches, across the dried-out bank to the wall.

After he had walked along beside the wall for a little while, he arrived at a place where some of the stones had tumbled down. Here he managed to climb over and found himself in a square covered with paving-stones where what he saw completely took his breath away.

He was just in front of, or rather behind, the magnificent marble palace. In front of it lay a delightful garden with a marble pool full of water surrounded by trees and flowering shrubs. There was no sign of drought here. How green and fresh everything was. There were crowds of people walking round the palace, men dressed in European clothes, women in saris of every conceivable colour — but there were also a number of strange people who were quite different from any others he had ever seen. He watched them closely and almost fearfully. They were tall and pale with faces that were a funny pink colour. Their hair was lighter in colour and even their eyes were pale. The men wore European clothes, but the women were wearing short, narrow sack-like costumes — so short that you could see their legs right up to their knees — fat legs, thin legs, bandy legs, straight legs. How awful they looked! Suddenly it dawned on him that they were Europeans, sahibs, tourists — such expressions had meant very little to him until now and now he was looking at them with his very own eyes! And what an ugly sight they were too. But he knew that they were powerful and rich.

Some of the women came towards him. He nearly died of fright. Did they live there? Were they going to chase him away? But they smiled kindly at him and said something that he didn't understand, and one of them took a whole Rupee out of her pretty bag to give to him. Quickly he held out the bowl that was hanging on a cord round his neck and another woman dropped a few coins into his begging bowl.

Yougga was flabbergasted.

"Poor child," said one of the tourists to another in English. "How frightened he seemed. He hardly dared to look at me. Did you notice his leg?" They continued on their way. Almost two Rupees! So it was true that these foreigners were rich.

Here was a good place to beg but first he must go and have a closer look at that beautiful temple. He hobbled cautiously over to the entrance where all the people were going in. Ah, it was so beautiful that it almost hurt to look at it! As he drew near, it became apparent that the white marble was inlaid with precious stones of every colour in the shape of flowers.

An array of marvellous, multi-coloured bouquets of flowers harmonised delicately with the green of the stems and leaves. The walls, the pillars and the arches were all covered with flowers. In the middle of the great room were two sarcophagi and they too were inlaid with stones of dazzling colours. Perhaps there were gods entombed there? No, they couldn't be, gods are immortal. They must be men, kings.

Then he heard a woman explaining something to a group of young Indian girls, dressed in pretty saris — she was speaking in Hindi and Yougga could understand virtually everything she said: "This is the resting place of the beloved wife of Shah Jahan, who, after having given him fourteen children, died in childbirth. He loved her so much that he wanted to build a tomb for her, more beautiful than any other funerary monument in the whole world. And he succeeded. People come on pilgrimage from the four corners of the world to look at this miracle of beauty and he rests here in this coffin. He called his wife 'Taj Mahal', the glory of the palace, and it is under this name that the palace is famous throughout the world."

"Taj Mahal, what a lovely name," thought Yougga.

Slowly he hobbled along a path beside the lake fringed with tall, dark green cypress trees, and stopped several times in front of the strangely dressed European women, making himself twice as hunch-backed as he held out his bowl. Each time he did so someone put some coins in. The contrast between the magnificent mausoleum and this poor, thin, deformed child who had nothing to wear but a filthy loin cloth, was so striking that none of the strangers could remain insensitive to it. Then suddenly an attendant came rushing towards him brandishing a stick. "Will you get out of here at once, you mangy pup — what impudence! How did you get in here, you little guttersnipe? Get out!" And he pointed to the way out, a great arched portal of red stone.

As the boy rushed to the exit, trembling with fright, the attendant at the gate shouted at him too:

"Where have you come from, urchin? Get out of here or you will have me to deal with!"

Yougga made off as fast as he could.

He followed the crowd that was heading towards the city. The road was long with his crutches, but at last he found himself in a very lively narrow bazaar street. In the short time that he had spent in the palace gardens of the Taj Mahal, he had earned almost four Rupees and Nirad had given him another — what wealth. He bought flour and rice and bananas and rice cake and a fat water melon for Nirad. It was certainly a good idea to beg in this city, particularly if you could discover the places where the tourists would be. The square in front of the gate would surely be an ideal spot. He had also noticed in passing that there were many beggars and merchants there. But they didn't appear to have the right to pass through the gate. He would stay in this city for a few days until Nirad had recovered. But would he recover? Sick people had been known to die of their illnesses. A chill ran down Yougga's spine at the thought that he might find himself alone once more.

It was evening and pitch dark when the boy arrived back at the river. He had had to take a different route from the one he had used earlier in order at last to arrive at the place where the boat was anchored.

Nirad was still sleeping feverishly and didn't know what time of day it was, or where he was. But he could still suck the juice from the water melon. Yougga himself ate a couple of bananas and a rice cake. It was too late to build a fire to cook rice. The moon shone with a pale yellow light over the river with its sandy banks. The air had become deliciously cool. Yougga looked up at the white marble palace. It had a dream-like splendour with its domes and spires rising towards the starry sky which, in the light of the moon, was turning to a pale blue.

Taj Mahal, the glory of the palace . . . and those foreigners, those strange people he had met. How Yougga

6 *The Holy Man*

Nirad was still ill, so ill that he had difficulty in standing up. For the moment there was no question of continuing their journey and so Yougga spent his days in the city, begging.

Every morning he washed himself as the Indians do, bathing in the river and then brushing his teeth with a small pointed twig and finally gargling to rinse out any evil spirits which might have crept into his mouth while he was asleep. This was what they had always done at home; this was what you were supposed to do. Then he would put fresh water in Nirad's pitcher — river water! — and try to make him eat a little while he himself had something to eat. Afterwards he would take the long road to the busy streets of the bazaar, keeping well away from the temple. He had noticed a number of beggars sitting or lying next to the portal, and they would no doubt be quick to look after their own interests.

He collected a little money each day, particularly near the Taj Mahal where the tourists passed to and fro. Often, however, he didn't have enough to buy bananas and water melons — the only things that the invalid could eat. But Nirad had told him that, when necessary, he could take money out of his purse.

One day when Yougga was standing outside the palace gates he noticed a holy man dressed in a yellow robe. He was sitting on the ground with his wares laid out on a tray in front of him. The things he was trying to sell were very odd and a group of curious onlookers had gathered in a circle around him. Yougga too, drew nearer. In the middle of the tray lay a shining human skull. There were also skulls of various small animals, strange insects, twisted roots, twigs, curiously shaped stones and little clay writing-tablets engraved with letters. The holy man explained that these things had magic powers, some could protect you from evil spirits, others could banish sickness. This monk must be a magician, a man in contact with the secret powers.

"This medallion will protect you from chest pains," he explained to one customer. "Only one Rupee, you should wear it on your chest next to your skin." The man bought it.

"Do you have anything to make me fertile?" a young woman whispered shyly. "I've been married for two years now and I still have no children."

He showed her two roots which had grown round each other.

The monk gave her a long explanation. He showed her two roots which had grown round each other in a close embrace. She must tie them on a piece of string round her waist just above her navel. "It has helped more than one sterile woman," he added. The woman bought the roots for one-and-a-half Rupees.

For a long time Yougga watched the wise man who eventually noticed the boy and asked him: "What do you want? I can't cure your crippled leg."

"No," stammered Yougga, shy of talking to a man like that. "It's not me, it's my adopted father. He's very ill; it's his stomach and his head."

"Where do you live?" asked the holy man.

"On a boat, beyond the wall," Yougga pointed in the direction of the river.

"Yes, I've noticed a small boat down there," said the holy man looking fixedly at Yougga. "I'll drop by this evening to have a look at him."

Yougga felt comforted at the thought that such an intelligent man, with supernatural powers, was going to come and see to poor Nirad. When the boy got back that evening, the monk was already with the invalid. He had undone his loin-cloth and spread a thick paste that looked like mud over his stomach. The holy man sat there and mumbled adjurations as he moved his outstretched hands backwards and forwards over Nirad, who followed these gestures with wide open eyes. Yougga noticed that the leather purse was lying next to Nirad's leg — and he went to pick it up quickly.

The holy man gave him a frosty look and Yougga blushed. He put the purse back next to Nirad who hadn't noticed anything.

"Your adopted father is very ill," said the holy man, "but I will cure him in three days."

Yougga nearly fell to his knees for gratitude and joy.

"Oh, wise and holy man," he stammered, "I am so grateful to the gods for my having met you and for your helping us." The monk had long, straggly hair and a beard like most of the begging monks. Yougga tried to meet his gaze. His eyes were dark and cold, not bright and clear like those of the holy man they had met in the banyan wood by the river. This man was more interested in the money he could earn with his peculiar wares, but if only he could cure Nirad with his secret knowledge, nothing else mattered.

He stayed with them all evening and Yougga cooked rice seasoned with curry for the three of them. Soon the moon got up, bathing the cupolas and towers of the Taj Mahal with a pale, mysterious light, and beyond it stretched the night sky with its thousands of twinkling stars.

Yougga gazed up at it full of wonder. "Did you know that the powerful Grand Mogul Shah Jahan built that palace as a funeral monument to his beloved wife, Taj Mahal?" asked the monk.

"Yes, I heard a woman saying that to a group of young girls," said Yougga, proud to be so well-informed.

"Well, now I'm going to tell you something that you don't know," added the holy man who like so many travelling monks, liked to recount stories. "When Shah Jahan had finished building that magnificent marble palace, decorated with inlaid precious stones and marble sculptures, and he had placed his dead wife in a sarcophagus, he conceived a daring plan to have a similar mausoleum built for himself. It was to stand on the other side of the river, just opposite the white palace, which it would resemble in every way except that it would be built of marble as black as coal. He started it and had built the long wall along the river — you can still see the remains of it over there — when his son, the arrogant Aurangzeb, led an uprising against him, defeated him and threw him into prison. The old Shah could see the Taj Mahal, his dream palace, from his prison cell. It is said that he spent his days at his high, narrow window but he soon died of grief and was buried in a marble tomb next to his wife. He never had a monument of his own but just imagine how magnificent it would have been with the white palace shimmering on one river bank and the black palace on the other like its reflected image."

In the uncertain light of the moon Yougga could almost make out a black castle over on the other bank. He pointed at it — but all of a sudden he was alone. The holy man had vanished, like a shadow. What a strange man! Perhaps he was a sorcerer. Yougga crawled into the bottom of the boat and lay down beside Nirad. On the following day Nirad really did seem to be on the verge of recovery from his fever. Towards evening he walked about a little on the strand and two days later he was able to accompany Yougga on a short tour of the town. They looked at the magnificent marble palace in its garden full of flowers — from outside the gates. The shoemaker's son was very impressed by such splendour and by all the extraordinary things Yougga showed him.

Nirad hadn't dared to ask the holy man how much he

owed him for his help, but he hoped that the price wouldn't be beyond his means! When they got back to the boat that evening, Nirad sat down on the sand, put his money in a pile in front of him and counted it — he was astonished to find that there were only 78 Rupees left.

"You've spent enough, Yougga," he said to the boy reproachfully. "Didn't you manage to beg anything?"

"Yes, I did," the boy assured him. "I went begging every day and I've hardly taken any money out of your purse, even though water melons are very expensive in this town."

When darkness began to fall and Yougga was sitting by the fire making chapatis, the holy man arrived. He was carrying a huge basket and he had his wooden tray slung across his back. "I've had a dream," he recounted as the three men were eating their chapatis. "The goddess Durga appeared to me and directed me to come and see you. This very night as soon as the moon is high in the sky we are to leave this place and travel down river."

Nirad was flabbergasted.

"Holy man, would you deign to accompany us on our journey?"

"Yes, who am I to contravene the wishes of the goddess Durga! There must be a reason behind all this. Perhaps I am to protect you against the onslaught of malevolent spirits?"

"You want to come with us as far as Benares, which as you know is our destination?" asked Nirad cautiously.

"Yes, of course I have been to Benares many times. It's the ideal place for a monk. Later I shall go on to Calcutta where I have a brother who has a tea shop but all that will sort itself out when the time is right."

The night was dark and very hot; the air was heavy and oppressive. Was there a storm brewing? Would the rains come soon?

The holy man took two betel-nut leaves out of his pocket and offered one to Nirad. He smeared a little lime paste on it and seasoned it with nutmeg. The two men settled down comfortably and whiled away the time before their departure by chewing this strong, fresh-smelling delicacy. Meanwhile Yougga cleaned the cooking pot with sand, then rinsed it off in the river.

Soon a light appeared on the horizon to the south and a blazing moon rose over the river.

"Let's go," said the holy man — he was called Pahari, the man from the mountains.

A blazing moon rose over the river.

Yougga pulled in the anchor and together they hauled the little boat across the sand to the water. Nirad grasped one of the oars, Yougga took the other and they drew away from the bank.

The holy man settled himself comfortably in the stern and watched the shadowy river bank attentively.

Yougga too, looked back. In the pale light of the moon, the light cupolas of the Taj Mahal were beginning to stand out against the darkened sky. It was like something out of a dream.

Nirad, who was still feeling the after-effects of his fever, was soon tired by the rowing and had to rest but Pahari got up and took over his oar. With long powerful strokes, he propelled the boat along at quite a speed. The little boat had never travelled so fast before. Somehow it was as if it couldn't go fast enough for him.

After a while Yougga also felt tired. It was late at night and he fell off the rowing seat into the bottom of the boat but Pahari calmly took both oars.

"You go to sleep," he said. "I shall carry on rowing for a bit while the moon is shining and lighting our way."

The Taj Mahal had disappeared in the darkness some time ago. Nirad and Yougga curled up together in the bottom of the boat that creaked and groaned under the powerful strokes of the monk's oars.

Soon they were both asleep.

7 *The Monsoon*

"This river is called the Jumna," explained Pahari next morning. They had moored on a sandbank to cook some rice. "It is a sacred river but naturally not as sacred as the Ganges. Like the Ganges the Jumna comes down from high mountains where the snow never melts." He pointed to the north.

"Have you ever seen the mountains for yourself?" asked Nirad, who knew only the plains around the large rivers.

"I was born up there," said Pahari with obvious satisfaction, because a man from the mountains always feels superior to a man from the plains. "It's a beautiful place. The steep slopes are covered with green grass, the air is fresh and scented with flowers. Tall trees with thick foliage provide shade and many animals live in the forest. But above the forests, huge mountains with their eternal snows raise their peaks to the sun. Up there lies the roof of the world and up there clear streams and foaming waterfalls rush down the mountainside. Water streams and gushes everywhere."

"Why did you leave such a magnificent land?" asked Nirad, astonished.

"Every man yearns to see new lands and new people," replied Pahari. "But when I am old I shall return to the lofty mountains."

The air was even more oppressive and heavy that day than it had been previously. The heat of the sun was almost unbearable, even though it was still only morning and sweat poured down their sun-baked bodies. Despite the fact that there was no wind, the air was somehow disturbed. Thick black clouds were beginning to gather in the south and west and thin flashes of lightning streaked the horizon.

"The rain's coming," said Pahari.

A terrifying flash of lightning tore open the clouds and a huge clap of thunder followed. The cloud banks built up rapidly. They had soon covered the sun and extinguished its light, producing a strange twilight that was quite sinister. In the distance they could hear an extraordinary rustling which seemed to be drawing closer very quickly.

"Let's get back in the boat quickly. It won't be long before this sand bank is carried away," said Pahari, who had assumed complete control.

They had just pushed off when the first drops began to fall. The three people in the boat let the blessed rain, for which they had yearned so impatiently, fall on their up-turned faces. Suddenly everything went dark around them and a heavy downpour began to fall from the dark clouds — the cool, lifegiving water felt marvellous to skins that had been dried out and cracked by the sun.

The pouring rain fell from the sky in sheets and made the water of the river rise, completely sweeping away the sandbanks. Soon the air was full of sweet smells — the delicious smell of earth and grass.

At first they relished the torrential rain which soaked everything including the thin sail-cloth stretched across the bow of the boat, and they laughed and shouted for joy. Little by little, however, the boat filled up with water and Yougga had to bail out. Nirad had to help him while Pahari rowed on regardless — as if he was in a hurry to get away from something.

There was not a dry stitch left on any of them nor a dry spot anywhere on the boat. Everything was running with water in the torrential rain. But the three men thought it was marvellous. Every now and then the lightning flashed and the thunder rolled but that was only a natural part of the monsoon rains.

The rain poured down for hours and eventually the three travellers in their little boat had had enough of it. They started to feel cold without suitable clothing and began to long for somewhere to shelter.

By this time they were surrounded by rushes; whole forests of rushes and reeds stretched out on both sides of the river. Most of them were dried out and half-withered, but it was already apparent that the water on the river bed was beginning to rise. Small streams brought more water down the river banks. Everywhere they looked, they could see water lapping and flowing. They couldn't set foot on dry land anywhere. They carried on rowing and the rushes in the swamp grew thicker and thicker. But at last the rain eased off and the sun shone once more through the scattered clouds.

Just as the rain had at first seemed to rescue them, so now it was pleasant to be able to dry out in the afternoon sun which didn't burn them but was content to warm them gently. The whole of nature seemed to come to life again after the refreshing rain. The half-withered rushes stood upright again, the birds sang and twittered and the three occupants of the boat wrung out their wet clothes and stretched them out to dry.

That day Nirad had caught some fish. "Fish bite best when it's raining," he said. In the end they found a kind of island of mud, onto which they pulled their boat, and tried to make a fire, but the reeds and the twigs were too damp. They had to make do with eating the last of the bananas bought in Agra, the city of the Taj Mahal.

As always, Pahari was in the know: "These swamps are called the crocodile swamps," he told them. "There are an enormous number of crocodiles round here and on land there is an ancient temple, where a huge crocodile lives with his own priests to serve him."

"Are there any crocodiles near where we are?" asked Yougga anxiously.

"All around us. You can't see them because they bury themselves in the mud, particularly during the dry season — only their eyes, their nostrils and the tiniest part of their carapace stick out. They look like old pieces of bark or a gnarled tree trunk. This is no place to go walking about at night," he advised the boy. "I used to know a man who had his leg bitten off just below the knee by one of those animals." And he laughed to see how frightened the two innocent villagers were. "Yes, well it's a good thing you have me with you on a journey like this; I really don't know how you would have got on without me."

Nirad wasted no time in assuring him of their gratitude.

During the night it began to rain heavily again. The chilled travellers were ready to continue on their way before daybreak. They needed to move to warm themselves up. It was impossible to light a fire because everything was running with water. Hungry and shivering with cold, they continued their journey through the crocodile swamp. The water had risen considerably since the previous evening and the island on which they had spent the night was almost covered with it.

All day long, wet and hungry as they were, they rowed and sculled. Nirad suffered particularly from the cold. He began to have fierce attacks of coughing.

Pahari arranged the sail so that it formed a roof and the water ran off it down the sides of the boat. It was a little drier too if they bailed out the bottom of the boat under the sail. That evening there was only raw fish for supper. "We must find a town where we can buy tomatoes and melons," said Nirad, "and where Yougga can earn some money begging."

"First we have to get out of this crocodile swamp," said Pahari; it was difficult to see which way the river was flowing in between the high reeds. The only indication was a weak current in the water.

Yougga kept an anxious look out for crocodiles among the rushes. Mouldy old roots moved curiously in the muddy water and Yougga thought he was encountering the malevolent stare of an eye under a heavy eyelid. He shivered. He was ill at ease in this place.

Rain, torrential rain, icy rain. Everything down to the covers under which they slept was soaked and unusable. It was useless to try and row in the dark because they couldn't see where they were going. All night the three men stayed huddled together under the wet sail without being able to sleep, their teeth chattering, and coughing.

Next day the sun shone again for a few hours in the

All night long they huddled together under the wet sail, unable to sleep.

morning. All around them the reeds were now fresh and green. They collected a small supply of twigs and rushes that had dried in the sun. That evening they would have the means of making a fire even if they had to light it in the middle of the boat.

At last they came out of the sinister crocodile swamp. In front of them the river stretched out wide and clear, shimmering in the sunlight, for even during the monsoon season there were sunny intervals every now and then. The rain and streams running into the river had already made the level of water rise and the current was stronger — which meant that they were carried along more quickly. So it was that at last, one fine day, they could just make out in the distance on the left bank the vague outlines of towers and large houses. It must be a town, a large town.

"At last we shall be able to go ashore," exclaimed Nirad, delighted. "There's a town where Yougga will be able to beg and you can sell your wares." The holy man stood up looking strangely troubled. "We are drawing near to the Ganges, the sacred river!" he announced gravely. "That town marks the point where the Jumna flows into the Ganges itself. I know that town. I've been there before. It's a well-known place of pilgrimage called Allahabad, but there are some wicked people there. We must avoid it. One of its inhabitants who is very powerful would like to see me dead — a curse on him now and during his next three incarnations. May he return as a mangy, hungry dog to be kicked about by everyone! We must row quickly past this town. Further on, along the banks of the Ganges there are numerous towns and villages where Yougga will be able to beg very profitably and where I shall be able to help some of those unfortunates who are in such dire need of my advice. For, as you know, dear friends, the gods have chosen me to bring comfort and relief to the grief-stricken and the sick — that is why I wander the earth in my present incarnation."

"The gods will reward you, holy man, for the goodness you show to us all," murmured Nirad softly.

Pahari sat down again and began to row vigorously. As they approached the dreaded town, Nirad and Yougga stared fixedly ahead, full of impatience and deep reverence. Soon they would see the sacred waters of the Ganges.

Allahabad stood on the left bank of the river but Pahari kept the boat on the other side close to the right bank. They rounded a sharp headland and saw before them, all of a sudden, an enormous expanse of water, a wide river shimmering, majestic, its waters rose-tinted by the setting sun. It was the Ganges, the most sacred of all sacred rivers, that lay before them.

Pahari stood up and stretched out his arms in greeting. With his palms pressed together, he touched his forehead and Nirad and Yougga did likewise. Pahari began to sing the old song intoned by pilgrims when they reach their destination after a long journey: "Oh, sacred Ganges, sent to us by the gods, we greet you and prostrate ourselves in the dust before you."

The indefatigable Pahari was once more at the oars. Now they were actually on the Ganges. Nirad scooped up a mouthful of water and drank it. How fresh and heavenly it tasted.

As the spires of Allahabad disappeared in the mist, it was getting darker and darker. A cool shower fell on them and Nirad had a terrible fit of coughing.

"Let's stop here for the night," said Pahari. He steered towards the bank and they soon found a quiet spot in a creek sheltered by a small promontory of land.

That evening they managed to light a fire so Yougga could cook a pot of rice for the three of them. The hot rice did them good, especially since it had been cooked in sacred water from the Ganges.

Then the rain started up again, but the sail which they had now stretched out to form a sort of roof over the boat, afforded them some shelter against the lashing downpour.

They could hear the waves of the Ganges surging around them and the water streaming past the little boat as it pitched and rolled.

"Shall I tell you why the Ganges is the most sacred river in all the world?" asked the travelling monk who was longing to tell the story.

The other two urged him on with enthusiasm.

"Centuries ago," he recounted, "the Ganges was a celestial river winding its way through the green fields of paradise and the gods frolicked along its banks, but the earth was as empty and dry as a desert. At that time the son of a king begged the gods to take pity on the human race and send the clear waters of the Ganges down to earth. They did so and the earth began to become fertile and turn green with luxurious plains and forests with thick foliage. That's why the waters of the Ganges are more sacred than the waters of any other river. They sprang from a heavenly source!"

Neither Nirad nor Yougga had been counting the days. Neither of them knew how many weeks, how many months even, they had been travelling. The three pilgrims in their little boat took their time. Once they were some distance away from Agra, Pahari didn't seem to be in quite such a rush as before. If the monsoon rains were too heavy and went on for too long, the three travellers would pull the boat well ashore and turn it over to form a shelter against the deluge. There they would stay for a while until the weather improved. Whenever they came to towns where the flights of steps leading down to the water were now flooded up to the top step, they paused for a few days and while Pahari laid out his wares in a corner of the market-place, Yougga would beg in the streets of the bazaar and Nirad would try to fish. He couldn't do anything more strenuous, for he had never really recovered from his fever. He was still coughing badly and even the magic Pahari tried on him — at considerable expense — didn't seem to be having any effect.

Throughout the dark, humid evenings when they could hear the waves of the Ganges surging under the violent downpour, they huddled round a small slow-burning fire and often Pahari, the wandering monk from the high mountains, would set about telling a story and the two pariahs from their small isolated village would listen with respect and amazement to the holy man's tales.

"The god of fire is called Agni, he is the son of Brahma," he told them. "Agni lives in the middle of the sun. Flames come out of his mouth. It is he who throws the lightning through the black clouds to make them burst and send the rain falling to the ground. It is also Agni who lights the stars in the sky and when someone dies it is Agni who consumes the body and reduces it to cinders, while the soul flies out of its disintegrated wrapping. It will be Agni who will consume me when my life on earth is over and that is why I sing a hymn to Agni every morning at sunrise."

"The moon," ventured Nirad, "what can you tell us about the moon? Why is it sometimes full and round and at other times all thin and narrow like a small fragile boat? I have often wondered about that as I sat in my boat on calm evenings at home, and waited for a trout to bite."

"Of course, I can explain that to you," said Pahari, proud of his knowledge of heavenly things. "The moon is called Soma and Soma is the goddess of all the plants

Angi lives in the middle of the sun and flames come out of her mouth.

that nourish and give pleasure to men, especially the juice that we call 'soma', the golden nectar which the gods drink and which makes them sing and dance. When the moon in the sky becomes smaller, it's because the gods have been drinking the golden nectar, but they always leave a little and this residue grows and increases until the moon is full and round once more and the gods can revel and drink their fill of the delicious beverage. That's also why humans hold their festivities at full moon."

Nirad and Yougga felt much more knowledgeable thanks to these explanations. Pahari also spoke of sinister things that would fill any innocent listener with terror and give them nightmares — tales of devils and demons tormenting and haunting people, evil spirits that took possession of people and stayed with them in the form of illnesses that consumed the victims and could only be banished by sorcerers who knew the appropriate medicines and the right incantations to cast them out. Suffering and death are part of our earthly existence. That's why the king of the gods manifests himself to men in three forms: Brahma who creates all things, makes the plants grow, causes children to be born and animals to reproduce, Vishnu who sustains and nourishes all earthly things and lastly, Siva who spreads terror and destruction everywhere he goes. Such is our existence on earth that we must die and be totally destroyed in order to be born into another life. He also told them about Durga, Siva's wife who was as black as coal and had eight arms with which to kill her victims. Her red tongue hung out of her mouth and round her neck she wore a garland not of flowers but of dangling skulls.

Nirad nodded his head in agreement. He knew about Durga, the bearer of death, from the terrifying image that stood in the village at home. Life was dangerous and at times incomprehensible. Man must never become too sure of himself. What a good thing it was that there were holy men who could explain the wishes of the gods to the rest of mankind.

At last the monsoon with its torrential rain was over. In a sky which was once more deep blue, the sun shone again, bringing warmth to the fresh, rejuvenated earth. The river embankments and meadows where the cattle spent happy days were green with lush grass. The fields were ripe for harvesting, the fruit trees were in bloom and the coconut and date palms were beginning to bear fruit. One fine day the three travellers drew near to another large town standing on the left bank of the river. A number of flights of wide steps led down to the river and beyond them rose a row of old dilapidated palaces and temples. Pahari stood up and gazed intently in the direction of the city. Wasn't it Benares? Then he made out in the distance a long iron bridge with arches that spanned the huge river from one bank to the other. That was the vast bridge across which the great fire-breathing metal carriages rattled all the time. Yes, he recognised that bridge! At last they had reached Benares.

"Benares!" exclaimed Nirad and Yougga excitedly, full of reverence and joy. They were going to stay here for a long time, perhaps even for ever. Perhaps too, they would manage to earn enough money here to be able one day to return to their village in triumph. When and how was still uncertain. Anything could happen in the marvellous holy city they had finally reached, after so many weeks and months of travelling.

8 *Benares*

Unable to control their impatience any longer, they rowed over to one of the flights of steps, where there seemed to be plenty of room. Right at the top of the largest staircase there were innumerable ledges and platforms with round straw sunshades and under almost every one of these sunshades there were men sitting cross-legged in a position of meditation. "They are holy men," explained Pahari, "Saddhus and priests."

Just as they were about to disembark and Yougga was standing in the bow, ready to throw the painter round a post near to the steps, a man came rushing over demanding furiously that they push off at once. That was his post, the mooring for his boat and no stranger was going to abuse his privileges. Trembling with fright they retreated. Obviously it wasn't going to be all that easy for strangers to go ashore here. There were people and boats everywhere.

They continued rowing slowly along the foot of the steps where many pilgrims were bathing despite the fact that it was late in the day. In the midst of them a number of sacred cows were walking about with great solemnity.

There were women washing their linen too, and groups of people clustered round several holy men, listening to their gurus, their teachers with great respect.

Now the boat was gliding past the place where the dead were cremated. Smoke was issuing from five or six elongated fires and the mourners stood in small groups and watched as the flames consumed the bodies of their dead relatives.

Those to whom it was granted to die in Benares were truly fortunate. Cleansed of all their sins by bathing in the sacred waters and soon afterwards cremated on the banks of the Ganges, their ashes would be scattered on the river. People who had died like that could be almost certain that their long and arduous succession of incarnations to lives of pain and suffering was now over. Those whose ashes were thrown on the Ganges at Benares would go straight to heaven. In Nirvana they would experience eternal joy.

That was why so many sick and elderly people tried to go to Benares to die. After all what did it matter if they fell down in the street and died in poverty and wretchedness if they would find peace and freedom after death?

"And that's why," explained Pahari, "the Brahmins who are responsible for cremating the bodies and selling the materials for the fires are often rich. The richest of them lives in that large palace over there," he pointed to a palace which was indeed huge but in a sad state of disrepair. Right at the top of it was a terrace flanked by two enormous lions painted black and yellow. This huge palace had once belonged to a powerful maharajah but all such princes had been deposed now and they no longer had the means to live in their old palaces. Now such buildings were occupied by private business men like the "prince" who presided over the cremations, or they were converted into inns and hotels for pilgrims of means.

"But where can we go ashore?" asked Nirad anxiously.

"We would easily find a place outside the town,"

replied Pahari, "but I'm wondering if we wouldn't do better to hire a mooring here even if it does cost money, because if we moor up outside the town and we all three leave the boat we run the risk of the boat and its contents being stolen by the time we get back. Bear in mind there are a lot of thieves and scoundrels in this city."

"How much would it cost us?" asked Nirad. He was aware that he was nearing the end of his money without really knowing where it had gone, and it worried him slightly.

"I'll arrange it," promised Pahari, generously. They steered over to one of the flights of steps and the monk leapt ashore. After a long discussion with a fat old man with a white dhoti and bare chest, he came back saying, "I knocked him down to ten Rupees for a mooring here for a fortnight. I think that's a bargain."

Reluctantly Nirad took out his purse and gave ten Rupees to the monk who promptly rushed back to the fat man and gave him five — the rest he slipped into his own pocket.

So it was that they could at last step ashore in the holy city. Everywhere in between the palaces, at the top of the steps, stood extraordinary towers and what a colourful life unfolded before them within the city's confines!

In a small square surrounded by temples and stalls a group of beggars were sitting on the ground — and what beggars! Yougga was disheartened by the sight of them. There were lepers with disfigured faces and hands and feet that were deformed and rotting. Some of them couldn't even walk. They were sitting on boards mounted on small wheels and their relatives had pushed them to this spot.

Old men, emaciated and almost naked, and old women dressed in the most pitiful rags imaginable, some of them blind or deformed, shared the square with holy monks, draped in their yellow robes. Sitting on their mats, completely absorbed in their meditations or their reading from the sacred books, these monks each had a shining copper pot full of water from the Ganges and a begging bowl beside them; that was all they possessed in the world. There was also a teeming throng of street vendors, offering all kinds of things in small bowls or on trays laid out on the ground: strings of fragrant beads made of sandalwood, sticks of incense, garlands of flowers to decorate the statues of the gods, magnificently coloured religious images — and fruit and vegetables too! There were shoemenders repairing old shoes and little shoeshine boys who banged their brushes on their boxes as they called out: "Venerable sir, if you want shiny shoes just come to me!"

Amongst all these poor people there were also pilgrims, some of them rich and well-dressed, others poor and half-naked, all of them, or nearly all of them, holding a little copper pot in which to take home some sacred water from the Ganges.

Pahari steered his two companions through small alleyways where the rich and the poor rubbed shoulders among the stalls offering everything and anything for sale — food, spices, copper pots and mugs, brightly-coloured saris threaded with gold, embroidered sandals, carved ivory, gold and silver jewellery and sacred images.

Numerous temples, heralded by the incessant penetrating sound of their bells, punctuated the winding streets and many people were going in to worship. Nirad and Yougga also went into a temple where they prostrated themselves before the terrifying image of Siva and gave a few Pice to the Brahmin who guarded the sanctuary. In return he put a red mark on their forehead. They took it as a blessing. Now they were really in Benares.

That evening Pahari took his leave of them. "I have friends here in the city, with whom I shall stay, but you will generally be able to find me behind the large temple to Siva — there's a small square where I shall set myself up with my miracle cures. As for you two, I suppose you'll be living in your boat? If you need my help, I shall always be at your disposal." Nirad thanked him warmly for all the help he had given them and Pahari disappeared into the crowd with his basket and his wooden tray.

After he had gone Nirad emptied his purse into his lap to count out his riches and to his horror found that there were only 20 Rupees left. Where had his fortune gone? Nirad and Yougga looked at each other in bewilderment. Neither of them dared to give voice to what they confusedly suspected: Pahari. But no, that was out of the question. The holy man had only had a few Rupees every now and then and he had earned them. After all, they mustn't forget that it was he who had cured Nirad of his fever and led them so competently to the destination of their dreams, Benares! And what about all those wonderful, clever things he had told them about!

"I must have lost some of my money — perhaps it fell in the water." Nirad decided not to give it any more thought. Whatever must be, must be. "Tomorrow you can start begging," he said hopefully to the boy. "And perhaps I'll be able to have a go at making some sandals." Nirad had had the sense to bring his father's old shoemaker's chest with him along with a last and knives. You never knew what might happen.

"Nirad, I would love to learn how to make sandals!" begged Yougga, who had a strong desire to learn something — it didn't matter what. In the village at home it had been his secret wish to go to school but it was very rare for a boy from the pariahs' street to go to school — and for him it was quite out of the question. However, it might be fun to learn how to make sandals. Even if he spent the day begging, he could work at something else in the evenings.

"We'll see, we'll see," said Nirad, for whom such a strong desire to work was quite alien. He was quite happy just to sit and watch other people bustling about. There was always something going on in this city which teemed with life. Perhaps every now and then he could catch a fish. If only he weren't so inhibited by the wretched cough that gave him a pain in his chest. It was strange that Pahari had been unable to find a remedy to cure it, but perhaps it was the punishment for some sin that he had committed in his previous life, in which case, according to Pahari, even the most skilful sorcerer couldn't help him. He would have to put up with his illness until such time as the gods chose to relieve him of it, which might not be until he was dead. There were worse things than dying in Benares. At least, in that way he would have no more reincarnations — all his suffering would be over. Even so Nirad had no desire to die straight away. He wanted to spend a few years in this extraordinary, bustling city and if Yougga worked hard at his begging, no doubt they could both come through quite nicely. Nirad felt that a bright future lay ahead of them despite the fact that they had hardly any money left.

9 *Yougga Learns The Art of Begging*

At first Yougga took his place among the other beggars sitting in the little square through which most of the pilgrims passed on their way down to the Ganges to bathe, but Yougga was last in the line of beggars and many of them were much worse off than he was so he hardly earned anything and Nirad was far from pleased. So he tried begging at random in the small, narrow streets where many strangers wandered about, and outside the numerous temples. For a while he did quite well outside the temple of the monkeys, which many tourists visited. The women in particular — the mem-sahibs as they were called — were the ones who gave him most. The temple of the monkeys was an odd little temple. Its columns and portals were painted in dark red and monkeys clambered about all over it. They were sacred creatures — many centuries ago this temple had been a sanctuary for the monkeys and the priests had fed them with the offerings they received.

Yougga whiled away the time by watching the lively, mischievous monkeys scampering up and down the carved pillars or sitting, basking in the sun, on the pointed rooftops. Sometimes a young monkey would fall on a visitor's head, but no-one ever dreamt of chasing them away. After all, the monkeys belonged there; the humans were only there as their guests.

There were also one or two lepers who had taken up

Yougga whiled away the time by watching the monkeys.

their stand next to the temple. For a while things worked quite smoothly but then, when they realised that Yougga had a special talent for melting the mem-sahibs, they became angry and made life so difficult for him that he had to move on.

One fine morning, as he was hobbling across a quiet square, he came across a long row of coolies who sat waiting with their rickshaws for customers (sometimes for hours on end). He started chatting to one of the boys, who had asked him just for a joke whether he would like to be driven anywhere. Yougga replied with a laugh that he would like to go somewhere where there were plenty of rich people and not one single beggar!

"Give me 50 Pice, and I'll take you to just the place," said the coolie.

"Where is it?"

"The place from which I work is right on the outskirts of the city, outside a magnificent hotel where only the wealthiest people stay. This morning I brought a very smart sahib here, but he didn't want to go back. Give me 50 Pice and you'll be able to beg there easily!"

"I'll give you 30," said Yougga who was beginning to develop a business sense, "but how will I get back?"

"You'll earn so much out there that you'll be able to pay the full fare back — perhaps even in a taxi!" laughed the young coolie.

Yougga couldn't resist giving it a try. If all else failed he could always take his time and hobble back on his crutches. He climbed into the shabby little rickshaw, which for the little beggar boy represented the ultimate in luxury. The coolie steered him through the bustling city on his bicycle and Yougga was quite bewildered by so much noise and activity. Some sacred, grey-white cows, one of them with a necklace of multi-coloured pearls round its neck, were calmly blocking the street and everything — rickshaws, bullock carts and lorries — came to a standstill and waited patiently until the cows had crossed to the other side. A little further on two wide roads formed a crossroads and on a platform in the middle stood a police officer in a smart uniform, directing the traffic. Yougga had never seen anything like it. People had to wait until the policeman signalled them to go. There was one group, however, who were not prepared to wait — some black pigs trotted calmly over the crossing and the policeman had to stop the flood of vehicles quickly. Even pigs had the right of free passage, much to the amusement of all the onlookers.

Then they encountered a man with three elephants walking one behind the other. The large, fat animals were walking cautiously past a row of houses. Their driver was sitting on the first one's head while the others followed on behind in a very orderly fashion.

Yougga thought it must be one of the most marvellous experiences in the world to own such a strong, intelligent animal as an elephant, and be able to ride on its head. A little further out of the city, the long road was flanked by small, dirty, tumbledown houses and open street stalls but Yougga didn't notice either the filth or the decay. All the houses he knew were like that.

They turned a corner into a wide road bordered with tall trees. Behind them were lovely houses standing in green gardens. At last they stopped outside the most beautiful building Yougga had ever seen. It was like a shining white palace with columns, round which twisted beautiful clusters of flowers. The building was surrounded by meticulously kept lawns and a profusion of flowers, and many tourists dressed in European clothes were coming in and out of it. Outside the grounds were a string of sparkling taxis, all ready to go, and a row of rickshaws. This was where the coolie's usual place was.

"There you are, you can beg here," said the coolie with an expansive gesture of his hand.

Yougga paused for a second. There was a guard at the entrance with a stick in his hand so he wouldn't be able to go through there. As he hobbled round the building, however, he soon came across a hole in the high hedge, slipped through it and began to beg right in the middle of the garden, among the mem-sahibs. All went well for an hour and the money clinked in his little bowl, but then suddenly a gardener appeared and he had to make off as fast as he could.

Once outside, he counted his money. Almost three Rupees, twice as much as he was used to earning in a whole day, but then the coolie wanted a whole Rupee to drive him back into town. They settled on 75 Pice.

That evening Yougga went back with three Rupees in his purse and for once Nirad was satisfied, so satisfied in fact, that Yougga succeeded in persuading him to get out his shoe-maker's chest, show him the knives and explain to him how the length of the straps was measured in proportion to the foot to make sandals.

So the days passed for Nirad and Yougga. In the evenings they lit a small fire in the shelter of a temple or in a niche in one of the flights of steps and cooked their rice and fish. Countless other fires were lit all around them and the pungent smell of smoke hung in the air. Many of the beggars and the poorest people had nowhere to live but the street, along the foot of the walls, but in summer the stones stayed warm after a long day in the sun and you could get by — provided you were in good health. If you were ill with nowhere to live and nobody to look after you, things could be difficult. Often all that was left in the morning was a bundle of rags which failed to move despite the fact that the sun was shining and people were walking past — someone had died during the night.

Yougga had noticed some women dressed in white coming past every now and then and examining these bundles of rags and speaking to them. A short while afterwards the person who was sick, dying or dead would be taken away. Where to? Yougga didn't know, but Nirad, who spent his days chatting to all kinds of people on the steps, told him that they were very good women who took the sick people to a place where they were fed and cared for. Yougga promised himself that he would follow one of them one day to see where they came from.

Yougga didn't succeed in finding himself a permanent place to beg next to a favourable spot, a temple or steps where the pilgrims had to pass. The older or more experienced beggars always chased him away. Nevertheless, he generally managed to earn enough small coins in the streets and alleyways to buy rice to keep Nirad and him alive, and sometimes even a little fish or some cheap vegetables. Yougga soon got to know the city from the begging point of view! He could often be found in the square where the taxis and rickshaws stopped to drop off the tourists and every now and then he would take a ride with his coolie friend to the luxurious hotel, where he usually managed to sneak inside the grounds and beg a few coins before being discovered.

He soon learned that on every feast day — and there were plenty of feast days in honour of the gods of Benares — the beggars collected outside the temples in a sad gathering of gaunt, sick people dressed in rags, to receive a free portion of rice. It was the remains of the rice people had offered to the gods. What was more, sometimes there was a little goat's meat in it, because when people brought a goat as an offering to the gods, they could take all the meat home with them, except for the head and lower part of the hooves which had to be given to the temple. That meat was cooked in large cooking pots in the temple.

Nirad never missed out on those occasions but his health was deteriorating. He coughed a great deal and had begun to spit blood. He spent his days in the shade of a temple or a house, chatting to others who had no more to do than he. Sometimes he would sit close to a circle of people who had gathered round a holy man who was interpreting the scriptures or recounting legends of the gods. Apart from the pain in his chest and that awful cough, he thought, his life was much more agreeable than it had been. He was seeing so many new things and he didn't have to do anything all day except gather fuel for the evening fire. Sometimes he even had the good fortune to find himself behind one of the innumerable sacred cows just at the right moment — cow dung made ideal fuel once it had been moulded into shape and dried.

On Yougga's insistence he had also set about doing a little shoe-making every now and then. Sometimes Yougga would bring back a piece of leather, some old thongs or a used sandal when he came home in the evening, and he was eager to learn Nirad's skill.

He often ran into Pahari in the winding streets of the ancient city where the holy man set out his talismen and amulets, and there were always customers about, eager to buy. To some specially chosen clients he also sold a kind of aromatic cigarette and some white powder in tiny little bags. These things he carried, hidden in the bottom of his begging bag. Pahari was a businessman of many parts.

Every now and then he would also turn up at the foot

of the steps to visit Nirad and sell him some miraculous potion. One day he announced that he intended to continue his journey soon to the great city of Calcutta where he had a brother with a tea-house — but that would indeed be a long journey.

10 *Hard Times*

Winter was approaching now—not a season of snow and ice like winters in Northern lands, but nevertheless one of cool winds when the nights were no longer as mild and pleasant as in summer. Round about the new year came the small monsoon, the winter monsoon when the hours of sunshine were disrupted by many days of cloud and cold downpours. It was a difficult time for those sleeping out in the open under the stars. At night most of the beggars vanished into their various hiding places, but there were always some who could find no other refuge but the street and they often died of the cold.

At least Nirad and Yougga had their boat for which they were still paying a mooring fee. The sail protected them from the heavy rain, but the cold and the damp permeated everything and even if they huddled closely together they were often chilled to the bone by the early hours of the morning. The hour before dawn is always the coldest.

Nirad's cough was worse and he often suffered with fever. He had recently become much thinner too. What else could Yougga do but seek help from Pahari? And what else could Pahari do but place more amulets on the invalid's chest and murmur more incantations — and take more money for his services? There was no doubt about it, Nirad was really ill. Yougga was desperate. Now he not only had to earn money for their food all by himself, but he also had to find fuel for the fire, cook the meals and look after the invalid in all kinds of ways. He had to sit with him, persuade him to eat, comfort him and generally cheer him up.

Nirad mustn't die and leave him all alone! He had grown very fond of his travelling companion. They really were like father and son, or rather like brothers. They had slept side by side under their cover full of holes. Together they had marvelled at all the wonderful, unexpected things they had seen and experienced in the unfamiliar world they had discovered. What would become of Yougga without his friend?

Suddenly, in the depths of his despair, Yougga

Plucking up his courage, he limped after her and tugged tentatively at her white sari.

remembered the women dressed in white. He wandered about the steps and the temples looking for them, and one fine day he spotted one of them in the street. Plucking up his courage, he limped after her and tugged tentatively at her white sari. She turned round and looked at him with dark eyes full of immeasurable warmth.

"My adopted father is ill — very ill," he stammered.

"Where is he?" she asked, and the boy led her to the little boat near the landing steps. Nirad was lying in the bottom of the boat. He had thrown off his blanket and was moaning with fever.

The woman knelt down beside him and examined him. Then she stood up again and said: "We'll come and collect him." Yougga's relief was boundless.

A short while later two men arrived with a stretcher. They put the invalid on it and carried him away, with Yougga following behind on his crutches.

Not far from the steps, in a small alleyway, they went into quite a large room. On the ground, sick and dying people lay on mattresses along the walls. Other women in white saris were caring for them. Yougga learnt that they were called "Sisters". Nirad was also laid on a mattress and an older Sister came and examined him. She shook her head with a worried expression. "Tuberculosis in its advanced stages," she said to the girl with her. "Nourishing food — warmth — drops for his chest. I shall speak to the doctor this evening."

Yougga squatted down beside Nirad's bed. Today he wouldn't go begging. He hoped the kind women would give him something to eat, and sure enough when they brought Nirad his meal there was a bowl of hot meat

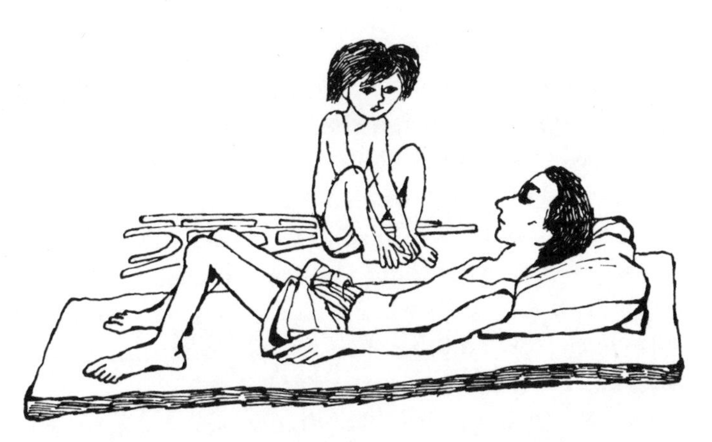

For several weeks Nirad lay on his mattress in the care of the Sisters.

broth with rice for Yougga too. In the evening the relatives went and Yougga had to leave too.

He spent that night alone in the boat for the first time since they had left their home village. It gave him a strange sensation of emptiness but he was happy at least in the thought that Nirad was now in good hands.

For several weeks Nirad lay on his mattress in the care of the Sisters, growing weaker by the day. Yougga spent most of his time at his side and the Sisters took pity on the crippled boy and gave him something to eat each day.

When Nirad was conscious they both talked optimistically about their future. When he was better, said Nirad, he would really set about making sandals and Yougga could help him. They would definitely be able to earn enough to be able to rent a little room to live in. They would have a proper workshop and a stone fireplace. Now and then Nirad would go fishing while Yougga looked after the shop. How easy life would be!

These conversations filled Yougga with joy — but in the evening when he went back to sleep in the boat, he was always a little frightened and concerned. Nirad's cheeks were so very hollow now and his eyes looked so strange and his cough seemed even worse.

Yougga would have liked to have been of some use to the Sisters, but what could a boy on crutches do? Then he thought of taking the shoemaker's chest to the hospital and every now and then he was able to repair a broken sandal. That made him very proud.

Pahari had also heard that Nirad was ill and in the care of the Sisters in white. Once he came to see Nirad and afterwards he said to Yougga, "They won't be able to cure him if my charms haven't succeeded. It must be his 'karma'! But when he dies, I'll take care of his cremation! I have the right connections and will be able to arrange it at a good price!" Inwardly Yougga was afraid that that was what the outcome would be, but he so much wanted to hope for the best.

One morning as Yougga went into the sick room a young Sister who passed him lowered her eyes and paled as she met his gaze. Yougga choked as a lump came into his throat.

Nirad was lying in his usual place, but what had happened? A blanket had been pulled over his head and he lay absolutely still.

Then the truth hit him: Nirad was dead! He knew it without having to ask. He sat down beside the covered body and touched it cautiously only to find that it was stiff and cold. Nirad was no longer there. He was dead and would never ever return. A cold, menacing sense of loneliness flooded over him and slowly he began to realise how difficult and awful it was to be alone.

Nirad had been a piece of home. Nirad had known their village, his parents, his brothers and sisters. They had shared the world of his childhood and they had been through so much together since.

Now Yougga was alone, far, far away from his family, compelled to fend for himself entirely. The little shoemaker's shop with its stone hearth was lost in the mists of despair. Now there would be only one way for him to make a living — by begging, begging until he was old with grey hair and a back bent double like the other old beggars who wandered about the town.

Nirad was gone! His grief was almost too much for him to bear. Then Pahari came into the sick room in his yellow monk's robes. He talked heatedly to the Sisters. Yes, he would organise the cremation. Nirad was a Hindu so his body must be burnt and his ashes scattered on the Ganges. He, Pahari, the monk from the mountains knew both Nirad and Yougga well. He was their closest friend. He had travelled here with them from Agra. He had at one time healed Nirad of his fever — but now Yougga thought that the mem-sahibs in white knew more about it than he did! This last was delivered with a sharp look at Yougga who was looking pale as he sat, huddled beside the body of Nirad.

Pahari had made the necessary arrangements with a man who would see to the cremation for a price which, according to Pahari, had been knocked down considerably. Everything had been arranged to the best possible advantage.

In a way Pahari's enthusiasm for organisation helped Yougga over the worst. "We must have a new, clean loin-cloth for him," said Pahari to the boy. "Do you have the money to buy one?"

Yougga didn't have a penny to his name. Had Nirad left any money? The boy didn't know. A search through Nirad's purse, still lying beside him, revealed only three Rupees and a few tiny coins.

Yougga remembered that Nirad had a new loin-cloth in his bundle on the boat. It had blue checks on it — would that do?

Yes, it would have to do, although a brand new one would have been better. "I'll take the money by way of an advance for the people in charge of the cremation," added Pahari, tucking the thin purse into his pocket.

Yougga had to go and find the blue loin-cloth. Then Pahari brought an assistant with a stretcher made out of branches on which they placed Nirad. The cloth was stretched over him and the whole thing was secured.

The Sisters patted Yougga on the head and one of them gave him a large piece of white bread and told him that he must make a point of coming back to tell them what he was doing, but they were delighted to see that he had such a good friend in the wandering monk.

So the two men carried Nirad to the place where cremations were conducted, where a small fire had been prepared for him. Pahari directed operations. "You can act as his son," he said. "You must walk round the pyre seven times and then set light to it. Just think how lucky Nirad is to have been allowed to die here in Benares and be burnt on the banks of the Ganges."

Yougga hobbled round the pyre seven times while Pahari recited the ritual words. Then the fire was lit. Yougga was pleased to be able to act as Nirad's son because he knew that it was very important for a man's future after death that he should have a son to perform the last funeral rites. There were many other fires burning in the small square beside the river and several groups of mourners stood waiting and watching. Some of the fires burned well and quickly consumed the body. They were the fires of the rich, made up of sweet-smelling sandalwood with melted butter poured over it to make them burn more intensely. The fires of the poor were small and burned more slowly. In the end the remains of the blackened bones and ashes were shovelled into the waters of the Ganges which had already carried away the ashes of thousands of other funeral fires.

Nirad had left this world. Darkness fell and a difficult day was over, but an even more difficult night lay ahead.

"Tomorrow I shall come to your boat," promised Pahari. "You owe me a lot of money, but we'll sort something out. Don't worry, I'll help you."

They went their separate ways.

Yougga hobbled down to the boat. Even though Pahari had promised to help him, he felt alone and abandoned, right to the very depths of his soul. Perhaps this was because, although it was a source of comfort to him that there was someone who knew him and shared his grief, he was a little afraid of Pahari.

When he reached the boat, he suddenly felt that he couldn't bear being all alone. He had spent his nights here alone for many weeks but then he had at least been able to console himself that Nirad was with the Sisters in white and that he would soon be well again. The boy sat down on the steps. A cool breeze was blowing and dark clouds were scudding across the sky. Something stirred behind him. He turned round and saw a dark shadow in the shape of a heavy figure on one of the platforms where the holy men spent the day. A cow, a sacred cow had settled down there for the night. Slowly he climbed the steps towards it. The sleeping cow seemed to give off warmth and security. With a deep sigh he snuggled up to it and laid his head on its soft sides.

The cow sniffed at him and made a slight sound. All night long Yougga nestled in its maternal warmth.

11 *Pahari Takes Control*

Early the next morning Pahari arrived at the boat. First he bathed in the river and invited Yougga to do likewise. Many other pilgrims were bathing along the foot of the steps. With arms uplifted, they glorified the blazing sun at dawn. Then the monk made himself comfortable in the boat and looked around him with a proprietary air.

"You owe me over 50 Rupees now, because that's how much the cremation cost, even though I got it at a cheap rate. But it was a fine and worthy cremation. Everything was done after the prescribed fashion. At least you can console yourself with that thought." Yougga was filled with sadness at the thought that he owed the monk so much money. How ever long would it take him to pay off that debt? He knew Pahari well enough to realise that he would have to pay it to the very last Pice.

"I have thought of a satisfactory solution which could be very advantageous to you. Listen to me carefully. We'll sell the boat — I'll see to that because I know a man who will give us a good price for it, even if it is only a worn-out old boat. Then I shall buy a rail ticket and you can come with me to Calcutta, that great city where I have a brother who has a tea-house. In a large city like that, there are many more opportunites, be it for begging or for any other kind of enterprise. You'll see, you'll easily be able to make your fortune there and I'll keep an eye on you."

Calcutta! Yougga was not without his reservations. If things didn't work out well, he would rather be in

Benares, the city he knew. But what he would have liked most of all was to try and return to his village to see his parents again.

"Is Calcutta closer to my village?" he asked cautiously.

"What's the name of your village again?"

"Kapuri."

Of course Pahari had never heard the name before and he knew that Yougga, the little beggar-boy on crutches would never find his way back to his lost village, but why not set the boy's mind at rest, particularly when it suited his own plans?

"Yes, Calcutta is much nearer to your village. If you earn a lot of money in the big city, you'll easily be able to get home from there."

With that, Yougga felt a little more inclined to go to Calcutta.

"When the boat has been sold, I shall be clear of my debt to you, won't I?" Yougga wanted to know just where he stood.

"Yes, possibly, but then there's the train fare to Calcutta. It's not cheap but we'll manage. We'll sort something out — just you leave it to me."

Yougga was not altogether reassured. "I shall want to take my shoemaker's chest with me and the blanket — and Nirad's shirt."

"You take anything of Nirad's that you can use. Perhaps I shall be able to make use of them too. We'll sell the rest. I've already found a buyer. You should be very grateful to me for looking after everything for you — believe me, without me someone could really take advantage of you."

Yougga sighed. He was not looking forward much to this journey with Pahari, of whom he was a little afraid. How he missed good old Nirad. Yougga had never been afraid of him. They had known each other for as long as Yougga could remember. But no doubt Pahari was a clever man who knew what was best for them both.

A few days later Pahari and Yougga found themselves on the platform of the large, dirty, noisy station outside Benares. The monk in his yellow robes had managed very adeptly to push Yougga through the crowds at the ticket control, without a ticket. Now they were sitting on the platform with a host of other travellers, patiently waiting for a train to come. Some people were asleep, others ate and talked, women breastfed their children and a holy man, unperturbed by the general flurry of activity, was sitting reading a tattered book. He had a kind, intelligent face. Yougga watched him for some time. If only he were travelling with that man and not Pahari, he thought, but that holy man was concentrating all his thoughts on what he was reading and neither saw nor heard anything of the people around him.

Eventually a train came into the station with a great commotion. The carriages rattled, the engine whistled and puffed out smoke. Yougga had never heard such a noise. Then people began to rush for the compartments, piling in through the doors and windows. It was important to be first to get a seat for most people would have to sit on the floor. Some even climbed into the luggage racks above the seats and small children were simply tucked underneath the seats, where they could sleep. Yougga had sat down on his shoe-maker's chest in the middle of the crowd. He managed to slide his crutches under a bench where they wouldn't inconvenience any of the other travellers.

The train gave a shrill whistle, jolted, puffed and ground into motion, and Yougga's heart raced with fear and excitement. He had never dreamt that he would one day be able to travel in one of the fire-breathing railway carriages people used to talk about in his village. No one who lived in the pariahs' street had so much as seen a train, let alone travelled in one.

Through the window he could see the wide, glittering river as they rattled across the long metal bridge over the Ganges, and then the train rounded a corner and the river disappeared. They were leaving Benares behind them and with some anxiety Yougga, who was not without a sense of direction, sensed that the train was heading East, while his village, Kapuri, lay far, far away to the West. Well, no doubt the train twisted and turned like the river. Pahari had said that Calcutta was not too far from Kapuri and he knew what he was talking about. In any case he would have to earn a lot of money before even considering going back to his village. By that time he would no doubt have long grown up.

12 *Calcutta*

At last they arrived in Calcutta. The journey had been long, dusty and tiring. People had got on and off and eventually Pahari and Yougga had managed to get seats. They had dozed through the long night, propped on the hard benches of the train. In the morning they had drunk cups of tea, served to them in earthenware bowls by a vendor who shouted loudly from the platform in a station where the train had stopped. It was on the evening of the second day that they at last arrived at the great city on the banks of the Hooghly river, one of the tributaries of the Ganges, which empties itself into the Gulf of Bengal.

The city of Calcutta, one of the largest cities of the world and possibly one of the poorest, sprawled out before their eyes. Officially the city had about six million inhabitants but it was estimated that approximately the same number lived there "illegally" in makeshift huts, in rough tents or quite simply in the streets. They were the poor people who had left their villages in the hope that they would have a better chance of earning money in this huge city, but most of them found only unemployment or badly paid seasonal work. Many refugees had also arrived in Calcutta at that time, the victims of famine or the war in Bangladesh which lies to the north.

The need in the poor districts was indescribable but Pahari knew very little about it and Yougga knew nothing at all. They were both happy and relieved to have reached their destination. It was good to be able to stretch their legs and take a walk along the platform after their long, tiring journey.

Noise, crowds, and dirt — at the ticket barrier a mass of people were jostling with each other to get out and an equally large crowd was pushing in the opposite direction to get onto the platform.

"I'll go on ahead a little," said Pahari to the boy. "You follow me and if anyone asks you for your ticket you tell them that your master and guru, the holy man from the mountains, is ahead of you and has already shown your ticket."

Yougga nodded his head in agreement. He was a little frightened. What would happen if the ticket collector wouldn't let him through?

Sure enough the man in uniform asked him roughly: "Where's your ticket?" Yougga blurted out what Pahari had told him to say and at the same time from the front of the crowd the monk in his yellow robes waved a bit of paper and called out in an authoritative voice, "He's my disciple! I am a holy man from the mountains and I've already shown you his ticket!"

The people behind were pushing and shouting impatiently so the ticket collector gave up the discussion and Yougga went through.

As they stood outside the huge station they could see before them the enormous iron bridge which led across the river to the city centre. On the narrow bridge the throng defied all description — cars honking, bicycle bells ringing, bullock-carts, rickshaws and an unbelievable number of pedestrians pushing in opposite directions. Pahari and Yougga were drawn into the crowd and carried across the river with it. Huge ships —

iron steamships — were anchored to the right of the bridge. Yougga gazed about him until eventually his eyes were exhausted. The city shimmered with the many lights of tall buildings and heavily congested roads. What a crowd! What chaos! If he lost sight of Pahari, he would almost certainly never find him again. But Pahari was careful to adapt his pace to Yougga's crutches. "Once we're over the bridge we'll turn right along the river. We're sure to find somewhere to spend the night there. Tomorrow I'll go and see my brother who has a tea shop."

They dragged themselves along the black, muddy banks of the river. Everywhere there were small tents made out of coal sacks sewn together and small hovels built out of cardboard boxes. Outside many of them burned small cooking fires round which huddled people dressed in rags. It was pitch dark by this time. In a recess between two storage huts Pahari found a corner for them to spend the night. They would have to wait until the next day to buy something to eat. Pahari smoked a couple of cigarettes he had rolled himself. Then they wrapped themselves up in their blankets and huddled together to protect themselves from the night wind.

The following day they continued in the direction of the congested town centre, where the houses were all squashed together. They went through a park and a large stretch of green common land, beyond which rose tall buildings. Here was the busy main street of Calcutta, flanked by a multitude of stalls between which rushed every conceivable type of vehicle including rickshaws drawn by thin, half-naked coolies.

The monk from the mountains paused and looked

around him somewhat at a loss. This was the first time he had been in Calcutta but he had an old scrap of paper on which was written the address of the famous brother with the tea shop. Pahari was soon tired of keeping in step with Yougga's crutches. He thought for a moment then revealed his plan of campaign. "First we'll go and buy some bananas from the market," he decided. They were ravenously hungry and wolfed down four bananas each. "We'll settle up later," said Pahari, as he took out the money. "One Rupee for eight bananas. Right, now I'm going off on my own to look for my brother. In the meantime you can try and beg round here — but I wouldn't try begging in the main street if I were you because I've noticed that there are already old men, women and children begging at various points. It would be better not to try and mingle with them, don't you think? But over there, where that wide street leads down to the yellow palace, there aren't so many people. Try and go down there and see if you can beg enough to pay for your food. Later we'll get ourselves organised properly because in time you're going to have to become a good beggar. At dusk I'll come and find you, let's say outside the big yellow building. There are sentries outside, it may well be barracks and it's easy to find."

"You will really come and find me?" asked Yougga, who was not a little afraid of finding himself alone in this large, turbulent city.

"Yes, of course," promised Pahari.

Yougga limped down the wide street with his heavy shoemaker's chest banging about on a strap across his back and his worn blanket over his shoulder. Obviously he didn't dare leave these valuable items anywhere. Just as long as Pahari didn't let him down and leave him all alone!

The yellow building stood at the end of another wide avenue where the houses were very big and very beautiful. The boy had never before seen such tall, imposing buildings. Most of the people, especially the men, were dressed in European clothes, and they all looked as if they were in a great hurry.

Yougga took up his stand, hunching his back a little more than usual and holding out his begging bowl. From time to time a coin was dropped into it. A little further down the road a splendid large building had a wide portal with a dais and two uniformed doormen. A string of coolies with red neckties were sitting in the street along the foot of the wall. There were at least six shoeshine boys on the pavement outside the house. Who, he wondered, might live there?

A car drew up at the portal, the doorman rushed to open the car door and the coolies stood in a row behind him. Out of the car stepped a handsome sahib and a mem-sahib, both of whom were foreigners with pale skins. They went through a revolving door into a large marble hall, followed by the coolies carrying their luggage.

It must be a hotel for rich tourists! Look how they lived! There must be plenty of money to be made by begging over there. A man in an Indian dhoti was watching the boy on crutches closely. Two foreign sahibs went past and the boy held out his bowl. One of them dropped a Rupee into it. The Indian stood beside

Yougga, snatched his bowl from him, and emptied it into his own hand. The little shoe-shine boys were watching the scene intently.

"Just don't let me catch you outside this hotel again, you cheeky rascal," hissed the man. Yougga hobbled away, frightened and disappointed. Everything he had managed to beg that day had been stolen from him! He would have to beg where there weren't so many people. Nevertheless he did manage to earn almost a Rupee by begging for the rest of the day, and on top of that someone gave him some bread.

There was no question of his leaving the area round the yellow building in case he missed Pahari when he came to fetch him, if of course he ever came. But Pahari had not abandoned him. At last towards evening, he saw the monk's yellow robe on the other side of the street. The boy ran towards him as fast as he could.

"So, have you earned anything?"

"Not a lot, almost a Rupee; but I ran into a horrible man who took everything I had in my bowl."

"The villain! May his body rot while he is still alive! You must realise that there are many wicked people in this city. Watch out for them."

"Did you find your worthy brother and his tea shop?"

"Yes, I found him, it's not a very large tea shop — really it's not — but it could be expanded. Come along, follow me. We can spend the night there."

Yougga was delighted that Pahari had not left him in the lurch. They went off through the overcrowded streets. All around them the lights were being lit, cars hooted to try and get through the congestion and on one

It was a very small tea house with a counter accessible to the street.

street corner a sacred cow stood and slowly chewed some dry straw. Yougga stroked her soft skin as he went past. He liked cows! At last they arrived at the famous tea shop. It was really very small with a counter accessible to the street, a narrow, poor street. Behind the counter a stone hearth was visible with a large boiling cauldron. The tea was served in small earthenware bowls, and for an additional fee people could have cane sugar with it. Pahari and the boy slipped under the counter into the dark rear of the shop where Pahari's brother was standing to serve tea. At the very back, his wife was making chapatis intended for customers. A roof over his head, a blazing fire, hot tea and chapatis — to Yougga, the little beggar-boy, it was heaven.

13 *A New Master*

Pahari was no longer wearing his long yellow robe and he had had his long tangled hair cut. He was no longer the holy man from the mountains. The next day when Yougga came back from begging with one Rupee and 60 Pice that Pahari immediately pocketed, he had difficulty in recognising his travelling companion. Yougga stared at him. Was this well-groomed man in a white dhoti and neckerchief really Pahari, the guru, the sorcerer from the high mountains? He now looked just like anybody else, except for the piercing dark eyes which were still the same.

Pahari had contrived a plan which greatly interested his brother. It would seem that the former monk had accumulated quite a sizeable sum of money during his extensive travels. His brother's tea shop, and the more peaceful life he could lead there, had long been on his mind and, having at last reached it, his penetrating gaze had noted immediately that this pathetic stall was far too modest for his purposes. Its position, however, in a small side street between two main roads was ideal. They must extend the shop and set up a small room where people could sit down to drink their tea in the shade when the sun outside in the dirty street was too fierce. His brother was quite carried away by the idea. He could sell iced water, orange juice and coca-cola as well. They would have to employ a girl to serve and help make the chapatis but there was no shortage of girls among the many poor families in the neighbourhood. Pahari would go into partnership with his brother and invest some money in the business.

Pahari counted his money. He had made more than 700 Rupees out of his many and varied transactions. His brother had only a small amount of cash but he had the stall and the customers. The stall next to his was a small shoemaker's shop which Yougga surveyed longingly. The shoemaker was elderly and alone, and he wanted to sell up, but he was asking 500 Rupees for his miserable room. The two brothers were counting on making him drop his price considerably. Then they would have to straighten the room out, paint it, and get hold of some benches and tables. On top of that they would need shelves and some wall-cupboards.

Pahari wanted money; in fact he had convinced himself that he actually needed it. His gaze fell upon Yougga. The lad must become a professional beggar — with his deformed leg he was born for it, so perhaps it would be best for all concerned if he were to go to a professional beggar who could show him where to go.

Pahari would sell Yougga to a professional beggar — that was the only sensible thing to do, and in that way the former guru would be able to add yet another tidy sum to his small fortune. His brother, who had the right connections in Calcutta, soon came up with a man who dealt with that kind of thing. This man employed three children and an old man who lived with him and in addition to that he organised the work of other beggars in the neighbourhood. The man, called Gopan — a small, very thin, pock-marked individual who wore dirty dhotis and a white shirt — came one evening to fetch

Yougga. After much heated discussion 130 Rupees were paid to Pahari who consequently considered that his commitments to Yougga were over. After all he had really done a great deal for this young stranger. He had brought him to the big city and had set him up securely as a professional beggar.

Yougga took his leave of the people in the tea shop and of Pahari, who wasn't really Pahari any more but some stranger; yet despite everything, he was the only person to have known Nirad and so to have belonged in some small way to Yougga's past. When they parted, Pahari issued a warm invitation to the little beggar boy. "Come and see us, Yougga," he said. "You can always have a tea or a coke here. You know our prices are not over-expensive," and the words were of some comfort to the boy. At least he knew someone in this huge and terrifying city.

Yougga hobbled down the street behind the stranger who was to become his adopted father, with a heavy heart. He was not sad, just frightened. He had already lived through so much and his expectations of life were very low. A place to sleep, enough to eat to survive, clothes on his back, that was all that the majority of poor people in this great city asked for. And it was all he needed too, but if possible he would prefer to be surrounded by kind faces.

Now he was going to become a proper beggar, provided it wasn't beyond his capabilities. He would have preferred to become a shoemaker but a man's future rests in the hands of the gods — his destiny, his karma was inescapable. Millions of poverty-stricken Indians consoled themselves with that thought.

They had to walk for a long time before they reached the man's house, in a poor, sad little street on the other side of the city's main road. Yougga tried to remember the streets but he soon had to give up. In the end they stopped outside a squalid little house with a tiny covered veranda, beyond which was an open room with a rough clay oven. At the rear an emaciated old man with a sore right in the middle of his face was sitting on a mat. Three boys were squatting on the ground. One of them had lost an arm right up to his shoulder. They were playing a game with pebbles.

"Have you eaten?" asked Gopan when they were inside.

"Yes," grunted the old man. They all stared curiously at Yougga. "I've got a new boy for you. His name is Yougga," Gopan went on. "He'll take Shanti district. But there's one thing you must understand above all else," he said turning to Yougga. His voice had suddenly become sharp and menacing. "I heard your former master invite you with incredible stupidity to go to his filthy little tea shop and drink tea and coca-cola paid for with my money! If I ever find that you have used my money to buy coca-cola, bananas or anything of that kind, believe me, I shall beat you to a pulp!"

Yougga trembled and the other three looked up, terrified. Gopan's expression changed and he tried to be more pleasant. "You cost me a lot of money — far too much money — it will take years before I get my money back on you so I want you to know that if you don't earn as much as the others do, I shall hand you over to someone who is much tougher than me! But if you're good and work hard, you'll be well looked after here with old Murti and your companions. Sit down. What have you got in that chest?" Yougga explained that it was a shoemaker's chest, and that his previous adopted father had taught him how to make and repair sandals. "Perhaps I could do that in the evenings," he added hopefully.

"Yes, perhaps you'll be allowed to repair sandals every now and then," said Gopan more amenably. "My boys usually go barefoot but perhaps there'll be something for you to do occasionally. Do you belong to the shoemakers' caste?"

"My adopted father was a shoemaker," replied Yougga.

"Well, castes don't matter anyway," said Gopan disdainfully, for he was a pariah himself.

Yougga sat down next to the other boys. He put his box in a corner and his crutches along the wall.

"The three boys are called Hori, Malti and Bola. Your master told me you've been begging for a long time and that you're a good earner. No doubt he was lying but you have done some begging, haven't you?"

"For nearly a whole year, since we left our village." Yougga's voice trembled a little at the mention of his village.

"Alright then, what do you say when you beg?"

"I say: 'Oh, venerable Sir, give a little charity to a poor crippled orphan and the gods will reward you'."

"We don't mention the gods much here in Calcutta. You've got to appreciate too, that most people in this city speak a different language from you. They speak Bengali and you'll have to learn some, otherwise people will not be able to understand you." Gopan began to talk Bengali with the old man and Yougga couldn't understand a word they were saying. As for the boys — he couldn't exchange a single word with them!

Gopan began to teach Yougga a few Bengali expressions to use when he was begging and the boys had a good laugh at his clumsy efforts but in the end he got it right.

"Now you'll have to learn the language the foreigners speak," said Gopan solemnly, with all the reverence of a ritualistic ceremony. "What do you say to the foreign sahibs and mem-sahibs?"

"I don't say anything, I just hold out my bowl."

"What you must say is: 'No father, no mother, no food — a Rupee!' " He spoke in English, then explained the meaning of the words to Yougga. "Come on, now you try."

Again the boys made fun of the newcomer's ineptitude but Yougga kept repeating the phrase until he had grasped it.

The boys slept in a small, dark room at the back of the house. They curled up sideways on a tattered old mattress in order to fit all four of them on. Yougga stayed awake for a long time practising 'no father, no mother, no food, a Rupee' until at last he fell asleep.

14 *Yougga, The Beggar Boy*

Next day Yougga was shown the streets in which he was to beg. He had to recite his two sets of phrases and was ordered to make himself look as hunch-backed as possible. And Gopan reminded him in a severe tone and with the very worst threats that he had no right whatever to spend any money he earned and that he must bring back every single coin with him in the evening. "Sometimes I do the rounds of the streets myself to keep an eye on you little demons and I take the money you've earned, so watch out!"

Then Gopan disappeared and Yougga began his trek through the long, dirty streets. He must have been walking about an hour or two and had only managed to collect a few Pice when Bola, the oldest of his begging companions came up to him. He looked quite threatening and said all kinds of things in an irritated tone pointing at Yougga's bowl and at his own. Yougga couldn't understand a word of it.

Bola tried again: "Two Rupees," he nodded his head happily; "Three Rupees," he looked concerned. "Four Rupees," he shook his head angrily and looked menacingly at Yougga — then he laughed: "One Rupee for bananas, coke. . . ."

Then Yougga understood. He mustn't go back with more than about three Rupees. The boys had obviously come to an agreement amongst themselves. He laughed to show that he had understood. "Three Rupees," he agreed and Bola disappeared.

He was made to recite his two sets of phrases.

He could have spared himself such considerations for the time being. On the first day he only managed to earn one-and-a-half Rupees, which put Gopan in a bad mood.

In the evenings the old man who was half blind used to cook a pot full of rice for them and sometimes they had beans or a few vegetables with it. Gopan didn't live with them. He lived in the same neighbourhood but in a much more spacious house which he shared with his mother. In the evenings he could often be seen in European clothes. He liked going to cheap cafés, particularly those where there were pretty girls. He also employed some rickshaw coolies and had a number of other businesses which were best kept out of the public eye. In fact, it was illegal to employ children as beggars and exploit them, just as it was against the law to sell them, but the police turned a blind eye to it all. Where else could they send all the poor, homeless children? There were far too few children's homes and they were all overcrowded.

Gopan was a harsh disciplinarian with his boys. They were pushed out on the streets early in the morning and they were not allowed to loiter about in the evening. If they brought home less than two Rupees, he told them off and threatened to make them go without their supper. The boys didn't like him. Rather, they were frightened of him and didn't dare to be anything but obedient. Old Murti was privileged. He had a fixed place to beg outside the cinema where people knew him. He went back there in the evenings when the last show was turning out but he spent all morning at home.

So the days went by for Yougga and the other beggars. Each day was just like the previous one and yet something new happened every day. It was hot again. The sun baked the little alleyways and a pungent smell of smoke rose from the hearths behind the open stalls of the bakers and the innumerable large pans of roasted peanuts. And in the roads where the traffic was heavy there was the unpleasant smell of petrol from the lorries.

Yougga was allowed to beg on a small stretch of the main street and whenever he saw a foreign mem-sahib, he would hobble after her, holding out his bowl. "No father, no mother, no food — a Rupee!" This was said in a sad, plaintive voice and usually the lady would drop a few Pice into his bowl, just to get rid of him — there were so many beggars along that road.

He didn't see Pahari again, nor the teashop. He didn't dare to go that far from his patch for fear that Gopan would come to see what he was up to. In any case he probably wouldn't have been able to find his way, but he would have liked to talk to Pahari every now and then because at least the former monk spoke his language. He still couldn't understand very much Bengali, only the most commonly used words, so he couldn't chat to the other boys and he felt completely isolated.

That summer was unbearably hot. There wasn't a single foreign tourist in the city. All the rich Indians left the stifling, stinking city and those who remained were irritable and apathetic because of the heat.

They were hard times for a beggar. Gopan was in a bad mood and spiteful because of the boys' poor results, and the boys themselves were tired and indifferent. Hori, the boy with one arm, caught dysentery and had a fever and Yougga was plagued with a rash and vermin. Old Murti thought he had caught leprosy because he had burnt his fingers several times on the fire without noticing and the loss of sensation in the skin was, it seemed, one of the first signs of leprosy. But none of them had enough energy to worry about it. Flies and insects were flying and crawling about everywhere, and everyone was longing for the life-restoring rains of the monsoon.

It was then that the rain poured down — with thunder and lightning that zig-zagged its way across clouds the colour of lead. The rain beat down in relentless torrents and people ran out into the streets with arms outstretched to meet its refreshing coolness. Rain water flooded down the streets carrying dirt and refuse with it and depositing it again in damp piles at the corners of houses and steps. Everywhere water flowed, streamed and spattered and soon the air was fresher and easier to breathe.

As the monsoon rains poured down, no one was left on the streets — the boys could no longer beg and Gopan's temper suffered accordingly. It drove him wild to have to buy food for a bunch of good-for-nothings! As soon as there was a brighter interval they were chased out to earn at least enough money for their food.

Eventually the monsoon ceased and then came the best season for tourists — the autumn, when industrious beggars could once again earn money. So the days, weeks, months passed. From time to time when people in the street felt that the shoemaker on the corner was too expensive, they would give Yougga a pair of down-at-heel sandals to repair and the boy would earn a few coins, trying to keep them out of sight of Gopan's eagle eyes. He had almost resigned himself to the fact that this was to be his life for how could it ever change?

Then, all of a sudden, something happened to transform the beggar-boy's existence completely. Gopan was arrested by the police. He had been dabbling in some shady deals and an accomplice had given him away.

When Yougga got back to the house that evening, little Hori, the youngest of the boys came to meet him at the end of the road. He seemed both excited and frightened at the same time.

"Watch it!" he whispered. "The police are on our trail. They've got Gopan!"

"Are they after us too?" asked Yougga terrified, for Gopan had always talked of the representatives of the law as if they were terrifying bogeymen and so the boys expected only terrible things from them.

"Yes, of course. They'll put us in a children's prison — or something like that."

"Are they in the house at the moment?"

"They've just gone but the police will take over the house. We won't be able to stay there."

"My shoemaker's chest!" lamented Yougga.

"You'll never see that again."

"I'm going to get it!"

"Forget it — they'll get you."

Yougga was desperate. The box with its pointed knives and its last was the only thing that had allowed him to hope for a better future. What was he to do now? Just then he had an idea. The residents of the street included among others a baker's family. There was a girl who had given Yougga a bread roll on several occasions as he went past the shop and gazed enviously in at the tempting cakes. She would help him.

He went to the baker's house and explained to the girl what had happened. She already knew that the police had arrested Gopan and that the boys would be taken away too if they were found. "Of course I'll go and get your box," she said. "You hide behind the counter so the police won't see you if they come in here."

Then she calmly went and took the chest from its corner in the empty house, and being a sensible girl, she also took a woollen blanket off the bed. "Thank you," said Yougga, looking at her as if she were a goddess. Indeed, perhaps she really was the incarnation of a goddess. There were people like that. She even gave them each a rice-cake before they left. Yougga would never forget the baker's daughter.

The two boys hurried away from Gopan's house and the street, where the police would be sure to look for them. That night, they slept for the first time on the

"Thankyou," said Yougga, looking at her as if she were a goddess.

pavement against the wall of a house, with a number of other grey figures around them.

"We shall have to go to another part of the city where nobody knows us," said Yougga next morning. They washed themselves at a tap near their pavement and then they set off slowly in it didn't really matter which direction — Hori with his one arm, Yougga on his crutches with his shoemaker's chest slung over his shoulder. En route they begged a few coins to buy some bananas. Hori was a puny little fellow, who frequently suffered from stomach aches and was generally not very strong.

By mid-afternoon they found themselves near a temple. A long line of beggars were standing near the entrance with their bowls. Yougga had witnessed such scenes before in Benares.

"It's a feast day in honour of the gods," he explained, "so everyone gets free food." They sat down among the other beggars, lepers and holy men. Next to Yougga sat an old Saddhu, a holy man wearing a dirty yellow robe. Round his neck he had a sort of rosary of carved wooden beads. He was reading an old, well-thumbed book. When he looked up his eyes met Yougga's and it seemed to the boy as if the sun was shining through them, the old man's look was so bright and penetrating.

"Doubtless you're on your travels like me, young man," said the holy man kindly.

"Yes, we've been walking for a long time today," said Yougga.

"And what is your goal?"

Yougga was a little worried. What was his goal? What was his greatest wish? All of a sudden, he knew.

"My goal is to learn something," he said, "to learn to be a shoemaker."

"That's a good goal," said the holy man, "but wouldn't you like to learn to read so that you could read the holy scriptures?" He pointed to his book.

"Oh, yes, I would love to go to school — that's what I'd like to do most."

"May you achieve the goal you have set yourself — that's what I wish for you."

In a flash Yougga recalled another holy man he had met, the wandering monk under the banyan tree, to whom Nirad had taken him on the first evening of their journey. He had used the same words: "May you achieve the goal you have set yourselves."

Had Nirad achieved his goal? He had died in Benares

and his ashes had been scattered on the holy waters of the Ganges. As for Yougga, he hadn't yet achieved his goal but two holy men had willed him to do so and there was power in the will of holy men — that was of course if they were truly holy and not like Pahari who charged so much for the help he gave and who was prepared to abandon his robes whenever it suited him. Yougga looked at the Saddhu with gratitude, but he was already deeply immersed in his book once more.

The door of the temple opened and the priests came out with a large pot of steaming rice. The beggars thronged round the pot and everyone ate their fill. "We'll stay here," decided Yougga and Hori was in total agreement.

15 *A New Hope*

The two boys settled in the area round the temple. At night they slept anywhere in the street — the heat of those sun-drenched days lasted through the night. Many other poor people and numerous beggars from the temple were also living on the pavement, among them even whole families with children. For them home was made up quite simply of a clay dish, a small charcoal fire, a cooking pot and a few tattered blankets. One night Yougga heard a young woman give birth to a child right next to him and one morning he saw some men come and take an old woman away. She had lived only a few steps away from the boys and had died a few hours previously.

Yougga and Hori had no stove so they couldn't heat their food. With the money they made begging they bought cheap bananas, peanuts and sometimes a roll or a rice-cake if they could afford it. They had been lucky enough to arrive at the temple at a time when there were plenty of feast days. It was "Kali-puja", the festival of the goddess Kali and on feast days the two children were sure to be found at the door of the temple waiting for a meal of cooked rice. In fact, it was next to one of the temples of Kali that they had taken up residence. Kali was the patron-goddess of Calcutta and Yougga had gone into her temple on several occasions with the crowds. He had seen the altar where the goats were sacrificed — the blood flowed into a gutter in the paved courtyard of the temple. Those making sacrifice must give the head to the temple but the rest of the meat which was now sanctified, they

She was the same black goddess who inspired such fear with her red tongue hanging out of her mouth.

took away with them. Yougga had followed the tide of people that flowed past the statue of the goddess and noted that Kali closely resembled the goddess Durga whom he knew from his home village. She was the same black goddess who inspired such fear with her red tongue hanging out of her mouth and the garland of skulls round her neck. In her eight hands she held knives, arrows and snakes and she was standing on a bleeding corpse. Naturally it was important to keep this vengeful, destructive goddess, who carried with her sickness and terror, appeased. Yougga offered flowers at her altar and received a red mark on his forehead from the priest.

Afterwards he saw the very old tree hung with small stones and bits of material, the offerings of childless women who in this way reminded the gods of their misfortune and asked them to help bring another child into the world, for an Indian woman incapable of bearing children faces a gloomy future.

One day the most unexpected thing happened to Yougga. Behind the temple there was quite a large building with similar portals and decorations. At one time the large room had been a hostel for pilgrims but it was no longer used for that purpose. Yougga had never really thought about what the old building might be used for now, until one day he saw a white ambulance stop outside the entrance. Two men carrying a stretcher got out of it. The covered shape lying on the stretcher must be a sick person. Then, out of the building came a woman in a white sari — a white sari with a blue border, which Yougga recognised immediately. She was one of those Sisters in white that he had known in Benares. So there were Sisters in white here in Calcutta too, looking after the sick and the dying.

From then on, he took a look at the entrance to the house every day and he nearly always managed to see one of the many white Sisters who lived there. Frequently a sick person was being carried in, and almost as frequently a dead person was carried out. Yougga was comforted by the fact that the Sisters lived so near. If ever he or Hori fell ill, they could always hope that the Sisters would look after them.

The feast days of Kali-puja were over, and with them the frequent distributions of free rice from the temple cooking pots. Winter was drawing near and the nights were becoming cooler but neither Yougga nor Hori, who by this time were used to sleeping in the street, felt the cold unduly. They suffered more from the fact that they had fewer and fewer opportunities to eat cooked food. Their eternal bananas and peanuts and the occasional bit of bread provided them with far too limited a diet and the two boys had become much thinner and weaker. Hori complained of pains in his eyes and problems with his sight, and he suffered almost constantly from stomach ache. As for Yougga, an angry rash on his face and chest had gradually turned into running sores. The fact was that the two children couldn't really look after themselves properly. They had neither insight nor money enough to get themselves a cooking pot to cook rice. Nor did they appreciate that they must try and vary their diet. They knew only that they didn't feel very well and that it made them bad-tempered. They had almost begun to miss their life with Gopan. At least then they had had a portion of boiled rice every night and sometimes some vegetables. Because of the excessive number of professional beggars round the temple, the boys had had to make do with the poorer streets in the neighbourhood where donations were small, but the temple cooking-pot and the knowledge that the Sisters in white were close at hand meant that Yougga had neither the will nor the courage to move to another quarter in the city, and little Hori followed Yougga like a shadow.

Then the winter monsoon arrived. Many of the homeless who lived on the pavements disappeared, nobody knew where. Others gathered where there was a covered portal or a porch roof in front of a house, if the people who lived there would allow them to stay. The occupants of the houses stepped over the figures lying outside and behaved as if they couldn't see them. What more could they do? Most of them were poor themselves and had only a small room to live in.

Having wandered about for some time, Yougga and Hori found a place under a bridge which spanned a canal in the neighbourhood. Here they found adequate shelter against the downpours, but the damp enveloped them like a wet blanket. They both began to cough.

One day when Yougga was hobbling down a poor alley some distance from the temple, he spotted one of the Sisters in white holding a little girl by the hand as she walked down the street and went through a gateway. Out of curiosity Yougga followed. He found himself suddenly confronted by a large room which opened onto a courtyard. Inside there was a crowd of children, boys and girls, sitting on the floor. Most of them were well-dressed but there were some in very poor clothes. On the far wall a large blackboard had been set up.

The children fell silent when the Sister came in. They waited eagerly while she handed out some small black square slates. Then Yougga understood. It was a school. He had never seen the inside of a school but he had often come across school children in the street. They were well-dressed and carried their books in a strap, and he had looked at them as if they were beings from a different, better world. It was true that in Calcutta relatively few children from the poorer districts went to school, even if it was said that everyone had the right to be taught. Poor children usually had to help their parents to earn a living

He sat down discreetly, half-concealed by a pillar.

or look after their brothers and sisters or else they lived with distant relatives who didn't bother about them or with professional beggars who exploited them. Schools weren't meant for boys like Yougga and Hori, he knew that.

However, since luck had brought him to school, he was going to take advantage of the opportunity to see as much as possible before he was thrown out. He sat down discreetly some distance behind the group, half-concealed by a pillar. Several children had turned round to look at him but the Sister hadn't said anything yet and there could be no more attentive pupil, no one more eager to learn than Yougga.

The Sister wrote some white marks on the board and the children copied them on their little squares. Yougga realised that they must be letters. The Sister told them what each letter was called and the children repeated it in a chorus.

Yougga, too, joined in the chorus as he tried to scratch the letter on the ground — it was very exciting. For a whole hour Yougga sat there quietly without drawing attention to himself. Then a man came into the courtyard pulling a small cart. It made a noise and the children began to fidget and turn round and chat.

The Sister said they should all go out into the courtyard and line up. The man put a large bucket on the ground, filled it with water, then added something white and the Sister stirred it so thoroughly that the water turned as white as chalk. Next the children began to go up one by one. Each was given a beaker full of white water after which they had a thick slice of bread which they ate while they sat and chatted. So this was what went on in schools!

Yougga went up in the manner of a beggar, holding out his begging bowl as he was used to doing. The Sister smiled at him and emptied the remainder of the white water into his bowl, and he drank it. It tasted like milk. He hadn't had milk to drink since he had left his village and the milk from the fine grey goat behind him. But this milk was extraordinary. It didn't come from a cow or a goat but was made from something white that came out of a tin. It couldn't be proper milk but it did taste delicious. The Sister also gave him a slice of bread and then she motioned to him to leave.

He went, but all he could think of all day was the

school, the letters, the children who could write and who repeated what the Sister said at the top of their voices — and not least of the milk and bread.

Next day he went back, quietly and timidly but full of determination not to be put off except by the person in charge. It was all just like the previous day. He sat in on the lesson for an hour. Then he was given some bread and milk and sent away.

On the third day he appeared with Hori. The Sister was hesitant. When it came to distributing the milk she looked at them sternly and was about to send them away but the boy with the deformed leg and a face covered with sores and his thin companion with only one arm roused all her pity.

"Will there be three of you tomorrow?" she smiled, as she poured milk into their bowls.

"No," Yougga assured her quickly, "there are only two of us.'

"Who is your father? Where do you live?"

"No father, no mother, no food." He was about to say, "a Rupee," but managed to stop himself.

"Did your father teach you that?" asked the Sister.

"We have no father, we're beggars, we have no mother either."

"Where do you live?"

"Under the bridge over the canal when it rains, otherwise in the street."

"With a member of your family?"

"No, we're on our own. There's just the two of us, we have no family."

"But you're brothers?"

"No, we just happened to be at Gopan's together. But he was arrested by the police. We're beggars."

"You're all alone in the world?"

"Yes, we don't know anybody else. We sleep together under the same blanket. And I have my shoemaker's chest." He pointed to the precious box that he trailed everywhere with him.

"Are you a shoemaker?" smiled the Sister.

"Nirad taught me how to sew and repair sandals," replied Yougga.

"Who is Nirad?"

"He was my adopted father for a while and then he died in the care of the Sisters in white in Benares. That's when Pahari brought me here and then we were with Gopan — but he was arrested by the police."

"You say your adopted father died with the Sisters in Benares?"

"Yes, they were good to him but he died all the same. It was his karma. And he was burnt and his ashes were thrown into the Ganges."

"And now you're all alone."

"Yes."

"Do you cook for yourselves?"

"Every now and then we get food at the temple door." The Sister knew that she had before her two of the innumerable nameless beggar-boys of Calcutta — children who were almost inevitably condemned to die in a matter of a few years. What was more, they were crippled. How desperately pitiful and thin they looked with sores round their mouths and ears, and those indescribably filthy loin cloths.

"You can come tomorrow," said the Sister. She wanted to speak to her Superior about these abandoned children. Yougga realised that he had won a victory. Now he and Hori had been given permission to come to school every day and learn and have their milk and bread just like the other children. Perhaps in this way he would even one day manage to read properly just as the holy man had said to him outside the temple of Kali: "May you achieve the goal you have set yourself!"

16 *A Great Change*

Next morning Yougga and Hori turned up outside the little school. They knew now that they had the right to be there. They had no need to be afraid that someone would drive them away and from now on they hoped to receive a bowl of milk and a piece of bread every day. Suddenly their lives had taken on a new sparkle. The weather was better now too. The winter monsoon had passed; the sun was shining brightly and with renewed warmth but it was not too hot. It was spring, the best season of the year, and there were plenty of other surprises to come for the boys.

After they had drunk their milk, the Sister told the boys that they could stay with the other children and they followed the lessons for several hours. The Sister began to tell stories about strange things that the boys had never heard of before, much of which they didn't understand, but Yougga found them even more enthralling than the tales Pahari had told them during those long evenings on the journey to Benares.

After school, the Sister told the two beggar-boys to follow her to the hospital behind the temple.

"We must put some ointment on your sores," she said to Yougga, "and your little friend must take some cough medicine." The Sister had already spoken to the other Sisters and told them what a pitiful existence the children were leading. At the hospital they went into a large room that was even bigger than the one in Benares. Along two walls of the room there were sick people lying on

She looked at the skinny, filthy boys with a look that was so warm, so intelligent and so penetrating that Yougga couldn't help thinking: "So there are holy women too!"

mattresses. Yougga had ointment put on his sores and both boys had to swallow a spoonful of cough medicine.

Then an older Sister appeared. She looked at the skinny, filthy boys with a look that was so warm, so intelligent and so penetrating that Yougga couldn't help thinking: "So there are holy women too!" for this woman's eyes were even brighter and more penetrating than those of the holy man he had met near the temple.

Then the woman, whom the others called "Mother Teresa", began to question the boys and she soon extracted from them the short but moving story of the two abandoned beggar boys, who had only themselves to depend on and who were too young to survive for very long on their own.

"We must find them a place in the children's home," she said to the Sister who was the school teacher.

"It's so overcrowded," sighed the young Sister.

"We must make room. These two can sleep on a mattress in a corner. They won't expect much, and they are both severely crippled. I'll take them with me when I go back."

Yougga and Hori heard all this without really understanding. All they understood was that someone was actually willing to look after them. They were going to be given food and a place to sleep. Beyond that they didn't think, for that alone was enough to make them very happy.

In a long dirty wall in one of the poorest districts was a green painted door which led into a courtyard where some girls were shelling peas and cleaning beans and laughing and chatting over their work. On the far side of the courtyard was a large house. The girls smiled happily at Mother Teresa as she passed. The three of them, Mother Teresa and the two boys, went into the house, climbed some stairs and entered a large room where numerous beds, both large and small, stood all along the walls and even in the centre of the room. In some of the beds there were tiny children. Other slightly bigger children wandered about in between the beds or outside in the wide corridor. Some were playing, others were helping the Sisters in one way or another; and some were simply sitting and watching.

"So this is a childen's home," thought Yougga.

"Sister Agatha," said Mother Teresa to one of the Sisters, "I've brought you two sick boys who are all alone in the world. We must find room for them."

The Sister looked at the boys kindly, but she was worried. "We haven't a single bed left," she objected. "What are we going to do with them?"

"They can make do with a mattress anywhere until we find a better solution. They're used to sleeping in the street."

The Sister sighed: "We'll do what we can!" Then, seeing just how filthy and neglected the two children were she exclaimed: "But first they'll have to have a wash!"

Two older girls took charge of them and they were washed from head to toe with warm water and soap. Their disgustingly dirty loin-cloths which were full of holes were put with the dirty linen. They might just do for rags," commented Sister Agatha, "but certainly not for anything else." Then she brought out of her cupboards two fine pairs of shorts, proper European shorts like those worn by the smartest schoolboys. The boys put them on with reverence. They hardly recognised themselves.

"You'll need some new crutches," Mother Teresa said to Yougga. "These are too short for you. Who made them for you?" "My father did," said Yougga softly. It still hurt him a little to think of his family at home in the village.

On the very first evening, Yougga set himself up in a corner of the courtyard with his shoemaker's box. There were many children in the home and they all wore sandals so there were plenty of broken straps and worn out soles. Seeing how industriously the boy worked to earn his keep, the Sisters arranged to get him some leather and thread so that he could do his mending. They called him "our little shoemaker".

That wasn't his only commitment, however. It was his schoolwork that was most important and no one could have been keener than Yougga to go to school. Every morning he left the home with the older children to go to a school some distance away. Their route led through one of the many poor, miserable districts of Calcutta on the muddy banks of an arm of the river, which had almost dried out and had been turned into a narrow canal. A large number of families lived there in whatever wretched homes they had managed to erect. There were hundreds, if not thousands, of pathetic hovels built out of boxes and scraps of corrugated iron, and low tents made out of coal sacks stitched together with old rags. In each of these miserable dwellings lived a family, often a large family, for Indians do not just include children in their families but also their elderly parents and other distant relatives who wouldn't survive on their own. They lived together in a single room often with nothing but the bare earth for a floor.

Water had to be collected from various small pumps in the vicinity and often women and children had to wait in a long queue for their turn at the tap. There were no sewers. People squatted down wherever they could, preferably near the river bed, and rats, flies and poisonous insects flourished irrespective of whether the sun was shining or the monsoon had transformed the whole area into a marsh.

The Sisters did a great deal of work amongst these unfortunate people for their needs were considerable, especially when epidemics brought sickness and death. They looked after orphans and abandoned children. Often in the early hours of the morning they would find a little bundle of rags outside their door, containing a small emaciated child whom no-one could or would care for. The Sisters also tried to take medical care to the sick and food to the hungry — and on the outskirts of this district they had set up a small school . It was there that Yougga and Hori went to school and it soon became apparent that Yougga was a keen and enthusiastic pupil.

17 *Encounter With the Past*

One day Yougga made a detour on his way back from school. He knew a place where he could sometimes buy a piece of leather that wasn't too expensive for a sandal strap, and Sister Agatha had given him a Rupee for that purpose.

Yougga hobbled down the little alleyway on his crutches. It was hot; a fatty smell from the baker's shop and the smell of the street vendors' roasted peanuts mingled with the smoke from charcoal fires and the stench of muck and half-rotten refuse.

Yougga surveyed it all with a strange sense of unreality. He had walked these streets as a filthy, skinny, wretched little beggar and now he was back, well-dressed, well-nourished and on his way home from school. The change had been too abrupt and he wasn't quite used to it yet. Could this really last? He didn't feel altogether secure. Would he one day end up back on the streets, all alone with no-one to care for him? Yougga wasn't going to worry unduly. He was used to taking things as they came, but in his heart of hearts he didn't really believe that these things could continue to be so marvellous, with kind, good people looking after him and providing for his every need. He was a schoolboy now. He was learning to read. It was too incredible for him to feel altogether at ease. That's probably why he was by no means astonished, only terrified, when he suddenly came face to face with Gopan on the narrow pavement.

Gopan, who was thinner and paler than ever — even a short spell in an Indian prison is no joke — stopped dead in his tracks in front of Yougga whom he immediately recognised and scrutinised with speechless amazement.

"Yougga! So here you are. At last I've found you. By the look of you, you have a new master. But what are you doing in those smart clothes? European clothes for a wretch like you! You belong to me — you know that to be true. I paid a lot of money for you. It was a very poor deal for me but you can start working for me again now. Just you tell me who your new master is."

Yougga felt a great gulf of emptiness inside him. He was trembling so much that he couldn't even answer. He had known it couldn't last. He belonged to Gopan; Gopan had bought and paid for him.

"Come on, boy, answer me. Who gave you those clothes?" Gopan cast a critical eye over the boy's clothes; blue drill shorts, a checked cotton shirt and a good pair of sandals. They would fetch about 10 - 15 Rupees on the market, and he could easily find an old loincloth to replace them.

"I live with the Sisters in white," said the boy softly. "I go to school." He was dangling his little reading book on the end of a strap.

"Let me have a look at that book! You going to school — what sort of lunacy is that? It's time you got back to work. I have a room where you can live. Old Murti's living there too. He has leprosy now but that's no disadvantage for a beggar. Have you any money? Get it out! Just one Rupee? Turn out your pockets so I can see you're not lying, you little good-for-nothing, you!"

Yougga did as he was told despite himself. He was in despair at the prospect of going back to Gopan and starting life as a beggar again, but how could he get out of it? Gopan had bought him, Gopan had control over him and he knew a child had no rights against a man. He could tell by the look in Gopan's eye which was lingering over his beautiful clothes that they would be sold at once and he would have to make do with a dirty loincloth. Then even if he tried to escape from Gopan at the first possible opportunity, it would be no use his running to the Sisters because they would be bound to ask him what he had done with the lovely clothes they had given him. "They've been sold," he would have to answer. "You've sold your clothes?" they would say and he would have to reply: "I didn't, Gopan did. I belong to him." And the Sisters would say: "Yes, if he bought you, you must work for him. We didn't know that. You have somewhere to live so you don't need to take up space in our children's home. Goodbye, Yougga."

That's what would happen. He might just as well give up now and go with Gopan. If only he could make off into the crowd and disappear, as Bola would have done, but he couldn't hobble away on his crutches. Gopan would catch him by the scruff of the neck immediately. There was no point in struggling.

The sound of drums and a frightening uproar could be heard coming from the end of the street. One of the demonstrations frequently held in the city was coming towards them with red flags and large placards — it was organised by a political party. Men were marching along the narrow street in ranks of three or four. Most of them had bare legs and were dressed in rags. They were heading towards the distant main road.

Soon there was confusion in the street. The rickshaw drivers rang their bells, the street vendors shouted and the drums were deafening. Lorries crawled slowly forward amongst the crowd, hooting as they did so. Gopan held Yougga tightly as he dragged him up against the walls of the houses.

Then a white cow came slowly ambling down the narrow street. The chaos was complete. No Hindu would ever obstruct a cow, for cows are considered sacred. The demonstrators parted and pushed to either side. Lorries and rickshaws stopped to let the cow go past as it walked calmly down the middle of the street. Its master had put a multi-coloured collar round its neck and its pale skin and large dark, soft eyes expressed a great gentleness. Its expression was one of trust. It had never been pushed or beaten or maltreated so why should it be frightened now? The cow surveyed all those noisy people calmly, but in the confined street the pressure against the walls of the houses had become so great that Yougga and Gopan were torn apart. The boy took the opportunity to hide in a courtyard behind a vegetable stall and, as luck would have it, the courtyard led into another road, from where he passed into other winding streets in the most congested part of town. Yougga hobbled away as fast as he could, casting anxious looks behind him, but there was no sign of Gopan. He had escaped.

"It was all thanks to the cow," he murmured happily. So he returned safe and sound to the children's home.

Gopan had lost track of him. Just so long as it stayed that way. When Sister Agatha asked him if he had found a nice piece of leather for his money, he blushed and stammered that he had lost his Rupee. The Sister gave him a funny look and it was even worse when they found that he didn't have his schoolbook. He had lost that too, he explained; but this time nobody believed him. Schoolbooks were expensive. Had the boy sold it and spent the money? The Sisters were no longer quite so certain about him. It was rare for them to take boys as old as him into the children's home. Most had come when they were very young. What sort of boys were these two?

It was as if the atmosphere round Yougga had cooled and he didn't fail to notice it. He felt even less secure. No, it couldn't last. It was all far too good for him. This wasn't where he belonged; he belonged in the street among the beggars, crooks and villains, among the poor and the homeless, but for as long as it lasted, he would make the most of it. He wasn't readily going to leave a place where he was given milk and food every day and a good mattress to sleep on at night, between pieces of material called sheets. Yougga and Hori shared a mattress in the large corridor which the children used during the day.

That evening, when the light had been put out and the boys were in bed, Yougga recounted his adventure to Hori, who was terrified.

"He'll look for us," Yougga told his little friend. "If you ever see him in the street, don't hang about, run away." Hori was lucky that it was an arm he was missing. His legs were perfectly good. It so happened, however, that one of the older girls who slept with the little ones was awake and overheard the boys talking, even though she couldn't understand it all. Next morning she told Sister Agatha that the two boys had been talking about a man they had met in the street, of whom they were obviously very frightened.

Sister Agatha was even more concerned. She was thinking of the missing book and the lost money. Was Yougga not really dishonest after all? She decided to get to the bottom of the matter.

Yougga and Hori were both questioned in turn by Sister Agatha. Hori was first and he told her about Gopan and the life the boys had led as beggar boys, but Yougga denied everything with all the obstinacy of despair. He thought that if the Sisters discovered that Gopan was his master, they would send him straight back. In the end, however, he had tied himself up in so many knots that he burst into sobs and admitted it.

"Gopan is my master. I work for him," he sobbed.

"Are you still working for him?"

"No, I escaped from him when he was put in prison but he's out again and I ran into him in the street. It was he who took my book and my money."

"Yes, but are you still working for him?" asked Sister Agatha sternly. "Now?"

"No, I'm here, but he wants me to start working for him again."

"What did you do when you worked for him?"

"I begged and he took the money."

"Yes, but why are you frightened of him? You're not begging any more. Why did you give him your book and the money? I don't understand."

"He wants me to start begging for him again," said Yougga. Couldn't she see?

"But you can say no. He can't force you."

"Yes, he can," sobbed Yougga. "I belong to him."

"But he's not your father?" This time it was Sister Agatha who was in knots.

"No, he's my master. He paid a lot of money for me, so I have to work for him." There, it was out! Now she wouldn't want any more to do with him. He would be sent back. But Sister Agatha was beginning to understand.

"He bought you?"

Yougga nodded.

"From whom?"

"Pahari."

"Didn't you know that no one has the right to buy or sell children? Only your parents have any rights to you but no doubt they're dead."

"No," said Yougga looking eagerly at the Sister, "my father and mother live in a house in a village far, far away."

In the end the Sister understood that the boy had been sold by his parents at a particularly difficult time to a wandering beggar — that kind of thing still went on — and that since then he had been passed from hand to hand until he had ended up in Calcutta, in the poor area, where so many human lives came to a tragic end.

"Would you prefer to stay with us?"

"Yes," his voice trembled with joy.

"Why?"

"Because there is food every day — and milk."

"Just for that?"

"And I would so much like to learn things."

"In that case, you can stay, Yougga."

"Yes, but what about Gopan?"

"Listen carefully. If you ever meet Gopan again and he tries to reclaim you, tell him that the Sisters have said that they will report him to the police. Then you'll see how he takes fright. He certainly won't want to have more dealings with the police. He's had quite enough as it is."

"So Hori and I can stay?"

"Yes, you can stay if you're good and honest and do your work."

"For always?"

Sister Agatha smiled. "I can't really promise you that, but you can stay until you can look after yourselves without having to beg." Yougga had unlimited respect for Sister Agatha. It was she who made all the decisions here. He looked upon her as a being from some higher world. If Sister Agatha had said that they could stay, then it was certain, as sure as a rock.

Yougga and Hori had a home.

No doubt it would take a little time before they were completely used to the idea but already Yougga felt, much to his amazement, that he was no longer frightened of Gopan. Gopan had no power over him. He was going to continue going to school and learn so many things.

And for a moment he recalled the blessings of the two holy men: "May you achieve the goal you have set yourself." Now he really had the opportunity to achieve it.

Glossary

Banyan tree: A type of fig tree.

Castes: Indian society was formerly strictly divided into castes and classes. It was impossible to move from one caste to another. A person was born into a particular caste and profession and must spend his whole life in it. The four main groups in the caste system were: the Brahmins (the priests' caste), the Kshatriyas (warriors and kings), the Vaisyas (farmers and traders) and the Sudras which included the lowest classes. These castes were in turn subdivided into a number of other categories. Outside the whole system stood the outcastes. On the whole they had darker skins than the Indians who belonged to a particular caste and they were often called pariahs or "untouchables," because those who had a caste must not touch them. They were given the most menial jobs. They swept the streets, cleaned the latrines, skinned dead animals and treated their hides. When India became independent in 1947, the caste system was abolished by law but the ancient traditions have not altogether disappeared from general consciousness.

Chapati: A thin pancake made out of flour and water and seasoned with salt and pepper. Chapatis are often eaten in place of bread.

Durga–Kali (Kali): Can undoubtedly be regarded as the same goddess known by different names in the East and West. This goddess represents both a creative and a destructive force. She is one of the wives of the god, Siva and is portrayed as a terrifying figure: black, with eight arms, a red tongue and a string of skulls round her neck. The lowest classes place great importance on the worship of this goddess.

Ghat: A flight of steps on the river bank leading down to the water.

Guru: A holy man revered by his followers as a teacher.

Kali: See Durga–Kali.

Karma: The Hindus believe that people have several lives. If a person does not expiate his past sins in this life, then he will meet his punishment in his next existence, for the gods never allow anyone to escape unpunished. This principle is called Karma. On the other hand, anyone can improve his Karma by being good and charitable and giving alms to the poor. Eventually a person can reach such a level of sanctity that there is no need for him to be born again into an earthly existence. This state of freedom and fulfillment may be compared with our concept of heaven.

Kengamma: An ancient pagan deity.

Kuli: A poor man belonging to the lowest class of worker.

Mem-Sahib: Lady. The term is also used for European ladies.

Monsoon: A period of heavy and prolonged rainfall. The summer monsoon occurs between July and August and brings heavy rains to the land which has been parched by the summer heat. Without these rains nothing would grow. In December there is another, shorter period of rain known as the winter monsoon.

Nirvana: Buddhists and most Hindus think of heaven primarily as a state of peace. It is the final liberation from the long succession of rebirths into earthly existences.

Rickshaw: A small, light, two-wheeled cart with room for two people at the most. It is drawn either by a Kuli on a bicycle or by a man running between the shafts in front of the cart.

Rupee: A rupee is worth about ten pence but has much more purchasing power in India. One rupee is divided into one hundred pice.

Saddhu: A holy man who wanders about the country as a poor beggar.

Sahib: Gentleman. The term is also used for European gentlemen.

Sisters in white: The Albanian nun, Mother Teresa taught for many years in a convent school in Calcutta, but she was so struck by the need in that huge city that she began her own work amongst the poorest of the poor whom nobody else would help. First she set up a few primitive schools and a "home for the dying" in the pilgrims' hostel mentioned in the book. Today she has her own order of nuns with some 3,000 Sisters. They do all kinds of work in the slums of numerous Indian cities. They run children's homes for homeless children; and clinics — especially for lepers. They distribute food to the poor, teach in slum schools and other secondary schools and do very much more besides. The milk they distribute to children in the slum schools is greatly appreciated.
The Sisters dress in the Indian way, in white sarees made out of coarse white cotton, with a narrow, blue border — that is why they are referred to as the "Sisters in white". Their official name is "the Missionaries of Charity" and their work has spread throughout the world.

Siva: The deity manifests itself to man in three forms: as Brahma, the creator, Vishnu, the sustainer and Siva, the destroyer. These three principal deities symbolise the eternal cycle of nature to which mankind is also subject: birth — life — death. Since Siva, the god of death is feared most, it is also he who is honoured most. There are also a host of other gods. Their wives and children, demons etc play a powerful role in the lives of the uneducated classes. India is a large country and every region has its own religious character.

Co-Workers of Mother Teresa in English-speaking countries may be contacted c/o the Missionaries of Charity at the following addresses:

149 George Street
Fitzroy 3065
Melbourne
Victoria
AUSTRALIA *(Australia and New Zealand)*

177 Bravington Road
London W.9
ENGLAND *(Great Britain and Ireland)*

235 Winston Street
Los Angeles
California 90013
U.S.A. *(United States and Canada)*

54a Lower Circular Road
Calcutta – 700016
WEST BENGAL

Co-Workers for any neighbouring English-speaking countries can also be contacted c/o the addresses above.